Roaring Fork

ROOKER

USA TODAY BESTSELLING AUTHOR

HEATHER SLADE

ROARING FORK ROOKER

© 2025 Heather Slade

All rights reserved. No part of this book may be used or reproduced in any manner whatsoever without written permission, except in the case of brief quotations embodied in critical articles and reviews.

This book is a work of fiction. The names, characters, places and incidents are products of the writer's imagination or have been used fictitiously and are not to be construed as real. Any resemblance to persons, living or dead, actual events, locale or organizations is entirely coincidental.

979-8-88649-398-6

A complete list of Heather Slade's
series and titles is available at
the end of this book or
visit her website:
heatherslade.com

Table of Contents

Part I

Prologue

Flynn
December 21

My heart hammered against my ribs as I stared at the manila envelope on Richard "Six-pack" Langley's conference table. I'd seen one just like it four times before. Once for each of my siblings. And the documents inside had irrevocably altered their lives, uprooted their plans, and forced them to follow directives from an anonymous trustee we now suspected had been appointed by our mother before she died.

I glanced around at my brothers, watching as they traded meaningful looks. All had taken their turns, sacrificing a year of their lives to save our family's ranch—our inheritance—by fulfilling obligations set forth in the Roaring Fork Trust. When their respective time was up, we'd been called to gather in this same office, hoping it was over, only to learn it wasn't.

With Holt's three-hundred-and-sixty-five-day stint recently completed, we'd been summoned again. I didn't doubt the trust had one final test—for me.

I twisted my wedding ring, thinking of Irish—the love of my life. While I sat, waiting to learn my fate, he was at home with our twin boys, Paxon and Rooker, and our four-month-old baby girl, Rowan Patricia.

Six-pack cleared his throat and adjusted his glasses. "Thank you all for coming."

"Let's get this over with," Buck snapped. "Are we here because we're done or to learn what impossible task our sister will be forced to do?"

The attorney pulled out a single sheet of paper. "I've received instructions from the Roaring Fork Trust LLC regarding the final codicil."

"Goddammit," Buck swore under his breath while I held mine, waiting for Six-pack to speak.

"It reads as follows, 'The Roaring Fork Trust further stipulates that Flynn Marie Wheaton Warrick, along with her husband, Paxon Warrick, and their children, must travel to Sangre Vista Guest Ranch in Taos, New Mexico.'"

My brothers tensed around me.

"Unlike the previous stipulations," Six-pack continued, "Flynn is required to arrive by December 23 of this year and remain until January 23 of next year."

"A month?" Porter echoed, disbelief in his voice. "That's it?"

I frowned, waiting for more. "What am I supposed to do there?"

"The codicil only states that you and your family must stay at the ranch for the specified period. No additional requirements are listed."

"This is suspiciously simple," Holt muttered, echoing my thoughts.

"Who owns this ranch?" Cord asked, leaning forward in his chair.

Six-pack shook his head. "I don't have that information. All I know is that it's a guest ranch, and you've been instructed to travel there with your family and spend the holidays."

The entire Roaring Fork Ranch—50,000 acres, the legacy of generations—would be lost if I refused what seemed like a simple vacation.

"Is there anything else we need to know?" I asked.

"Only that all expenses are being covered by the trustee. You'll find a confirmation email in your inbox with the details." Six-pack paused, his expression thoughtful. "I will say, this codicil feels different from the others."

Buck stood. "Then, we're done here."

"Thank you," I said to Six-pack before filing out of the office and onto the sidewalk, where my brothers formed a protective circle around me. Snow had begun to fall, the flakes catching in my hair.

"This is weird," I said once we were out of earshot. "Why would I only need to stay a month when all of you had to commit to a full year?"

"And why New Mexico?" Porter added.

Cord rubbed his chin. "When I had to spend my year in New York, it turned out there was a family connection through Mom that none of us knew about."

"You think there's someone connected to us at this ranch?" I asked as we walked to our vehicles.

"Let's talk about this at home," Buck said, motioning for me to ride with him and instructing Cord and Porter to go with Holt.

I was ten when my oldest brother left Colorado—then believing it was for good. So it wasn't until three years ago, when he received instructions from the first codicil, demanding that he spend a year living on our ranch, that he and I really got to know each other. Now, I spoke with him almost daily. Especially since his son and my twins were the same age.

"What are you thinking?" I asked a few minutes into our drive.

"The Roaring Fork Trust was registered in New Mexico."

"I forgot all about that." I gasped and looked at him with wide eyes. "Do you think my being summoned there has anything to do with the mystery trustee?"

He shrugged. "Maybe."

"Six-pack did say 'the final codicil.' It could mean they're ready to reveal themselves."

"I'd like to think so," Buck said. "Not that anything else to do with it has been that simple."

When we reached the ranch house before our brothers did, Irish was waiting on the porch, holding Rooker while Paxon toddled around his feet. My heart swelled at the sight of them.

"What happened?" he asked.

"It's almost too good to be true," I said as we went inside. "We have to spend a month on a ranch in New Mexico. Oh, and we have to leave in two days."

My husband's eyebrows flared. "Two days? That means we'll be there for Christmas."

"And New Year's."

"What's the name of the place?" he asked, opening his laptop.

"Sangre Vista Guest Ranch." I looked over his shoulder when he pulled up the website. "Wow," I said at the same time Holt, Cord, Porter, and Buck walked in.

"Wow, what?" Cord asked.

We all huddled around Irish as he scrolled through the photos. The property was nestled in the mountains outside Taos and had luxury cabins, gourmet dining, spa services, and horseback riding—it looked like something from a travel magazine.

"Well, sis," Buck said with a warm smile, "I don't know what this is all about, but at least the place looks nice. I guess it'll be up to us to hold things together here while you're gone."

I rolled my eyes at him. "Like any of you would have complained about a month-long vacation."

"Would have been nice," Porter agreed, chuckling. "But we're just glad yours seems shorter than what we went through."

Despite their teasing, we all knew one thing for certain—this wasn't just about a vacation. The trust had been orchestrating our lives too carefully for that.

Later that day, my sisters-in-law joined us for a family dinner. The thought that I wouldn't be with them on Christmas Eve or Day made me weepy. Last year was the first time we all spent the holiday together, and it had been the kind of family celebration I used to dream about as a kid.

"So, New Mexico," said Irish. "Has anyone in your family ever mentioned connections there?"

Buck repeated what he'd said earlier about the trust being registered there. "That's the reason the trustee can legally remain anonymous. It's one of the only states that allows it."

Irish nodded. "We should check with Decker Ashford and see if he can dig up anything on this ranch."

I'd met the man a few times, but hadn't really had many conversations with him. All I knew was that if you wanted information about anyone or anything, he could usually get his hands on it. According to Irish, the guy was rumored to be a tech genius in the world of intelligence.

"Already on it," Buck said, phone to his ear. "Hey, Deck. Need a favor…"

I opened my laptop to check the email Six-pack had mentioned. Sure enough, there was a reservation confirmation for a three-bedroom luxury cabin at Sangre Vista, all expenses paid, from December 23 to January 23.

"Two days isn't much time," I murmured.

Irish squeezed my hand. "We'll be ready. I can pack the boys and me tonight."

Three years ago, when the trust first revealed itself, I never could have imagined being married, with twin boys. Now, I couldn't envision facing this without them.

"What do you think is waiting for us there?" I asked softly.

Irish's eyes met mine. "I don't know. But your brothers all found something they needed while fulfilling their obligations. Maybe you will too."

"Well," I said, standing and lifting Rooker from Irish's arms. "Whatever's waiting for us at this swanky place, I've got a day and a night to prepare. And, honestly, if all I have to do is spend a month at a luxury ranch with my family to save our inheritance, I think I can manage that."

My brothers laughed, but their eyes held the same question I knew was in mine.

What was really waiting for us at Sangre Vista Guest Ranch?

I had the strangest feeling that this trip would finally give us answers—not just about the trust, but about secrets that had been hidden for years. Something about the way Six-pack had called this codicil "different" made my skin prickle with anticipation.

Whoever this mysterious trustee was, I had the unsettling certainty that our time in New Mexico would reveal more than any of us was prepared for.

1

Standing on the wraparound porch of Sangre Vista's main lodge, I watched the road that wound through the pines toward the entrance gate. The December air bit through my sheepskin jacket, carrying the scent of pine and the promise of more snow before evening.

Today was important. The Warrick family would be arriving this afternoon, and everything needed to be ready.

I pulled my jacket tighter and began my morning rounds. The walkways around the lodge had been cleared and salted twice since yesterday's snowfall. Ice could form quickly at this elevation, and the last thing I wanted was a guest taking a fall.

Inside the lodge, I made my way through the great room, where overnight embers still glowed in the massive stone hearth. I added fresh logs, watching as flames caught and danced against the river-rock chimney that stretched two stories to the vaulted ceiling.

Fresh wreaths and evergreen garlands adorned the main entrance, and pathway lights created pools of warm illumination leading to the guest cabins.

My boots crunched through snow when I walked to the stable complex at seven. Inside, twenty-six horses stirred in their stalls, some already munching hay.

Rick, our stable manager, looked up from where he was measuring grain into buckets, pushing his hat back on his graying head.

"Morning, JW. You're here early."

"I wanted to check the road conditions before our guests arrive," I said, though we both knew I could have done that with a phone call to the county highway department. "How are the horses this morning?"

"Good to go. Kit and Carson are ready for sleigh work if you need them, and the riding horses are sound. Weather's supposed to hold for the next few days."

I walked down the center aisle, checking each stall. Fantasma, our quarter horse stallion, stretched his neck over the door for attention. I obliged, running my hand along his neck while he snuffled at my jacket pockets, hoping for treats.

"The new guests have young children. Twin boys, about three years old, and an infant daughter."

Rick nodded. "I'll keep the gentler horses close to the barn. Maybe set up some supervised visits if the boys are interested. Kids that age love seeing the big animals, even if they're too small to ride."

"Good thinking. And, Rick?" I paused at the stable door. "This family is important. I want everything to go smoothly."

"You got it, JW. We'll treat them well."

Walking back toward the lodge, I detoured through the equipment barn, where Michael, our maintenance guy, was already at work.

"Morning, Michael. Everything running okay?"

"Yeah, all good. Pueblo Moon's holding temp fine."

"Good. I want you to do another walk-through this morning—check the faucets, test the lights, and make sure the fireplace is working right."

"Already on my list," Michael said. "Anything else?"

"They have small children. I want child-safety latches on the lower kitchen cabinets and outlet covers throughout. Also, check for sharp corners at toddler height and loose rugs that could cause slips."

"I'll have everything childproofed within the hour."

By seven-fifteen, I was reviewing the day's schedule with Sarah, our front-desk manager.

"The Warrick family's file," I said.

She pulled up the reservation on her screen. "Party of five, arriving today. Welcome packet ready with maps, activity schedules, and emergency contacts."

"What about their special requests?"

"Organic milk, decaffeinated coffee always available, and family-friendly meal options. Chef Alton has everything ready."

"Weather can be unpredictable in December. Make sure we have plenty of indoor activities ready—books, games, maybe coordinate with the kitchen for some cookie-decorating sessions if the boys get restless."

"Should I handle check-in when they arrive?"

"No, I'll greet them personally. But please be available in case they need immediate assistance."

At eight, I convened the morning staff meeting in the main dining room.

"Good morning, everyone," I began, consulting my notes. "Today, we welcome our only guests for the next month. We're closing the ranch to all other reservations during their stay."

Alton leaned forward. "Any dietary stuff?"

"Simple finger foods for the children—they'll prefer familiar options. We'll check with the mother in the event she needs anything special for the baby."

"I'll prepare a welcome basket with local honey and some of my softer cookies for the kids."

Our activities director, Lisa, raised her hand. "Shall I look into activities for the toddlers, or do you have something specific in mind?"

"The boys might enjoy seeing the horses, though they're far too young for riding. Supervised visits to the stable, maybe some gentle interaction with our calmer animals. Sleigh rides if weather permits, but with extra blankets and shortened routes."

"What about hiking trails?" she asked.

"Unlikely with an infant and toddlers, but the easier paths around the lodge might work for short family walks."

Jim, the head of security, spoke from his position near the door. "Any specific considerations on my end?"

"Privacy is essential. No staff should approach their cabin unless requested. All maintenance and housekeeping should be coordinated in advance."

I noticed the questioning looks my staff exchanged when they thought I wasn't watching. In the years since I'd transformed Sangre Vista from a working ranch into a luxury guest operation, I'd built a reputation for high standards but reasonable expectations.

But today felt different. Today required my personal attention in ways I couldn't explain to my employees.

After the meeting ended, my next stop was Pueblo Moon itself, situated on a ridge overlooking the valley. It offered breathtaking views while maintaining privacy from the other accommodations.

Michael was already there with his toolkit. "Latches are installed," he reported. "I've also added padding to the corners of that coffee table—it's the height where a running toddler might hit his head."

The main living area was spacious and welcoming, with a stone fireplace flanked by comfortable leather furniture. Large windows framed the mountain vista, while warm wood floors were softened by thick woolen rugs.

"I also set up the baby crib in the third bedroom," Michael continued.

I walked through each room. In the master bedroom, fresh flowers sat on the dresser, beside a bottle of sparkling cider and gourmet chocolates—adult treats to balance the child-focused preparations.

The second bedroom had been transformed into a welcoming children's space. Twin beds with colorful quilts faced a window overlooking the stable complex. Between the beds sat a basket of toys—wooden horses, picture books, and soft building blocks designed for small hands.

Cora, our head of housekeeping, entered with an armload of supplies.

"May I help?" I asked.

"I'm all set, JW. I've stocked the refrigerator, and Sarah will check with the family at arrival about how often they'd like housekeeping."

"Outstanding work."

She paused in the doorway, her expression thoughtful. "Javier? Is there anything else you want to tell us about these particular guests?" In fifteen years of working together, Cora had developed an ability to read my moods and motivations.

"Every guest who chooses Sangre Vista deserves our best efforts. Some require more coordination than others when traveling with small children."

She raised a brow, but wisely let it go. "Oh, by the way, Sarah asked me to mention that the Warricks sent a message saying they expect to arrive around two o'clock."

At one forty-five, I positioned myself on the lodge's front porch with paperwork I pretended to review. Fifteen minutes later, I spotted movement through the trees. A black SUV appeared, navigating the curves with the attention of drivers familiar with mountain terrain. As it drew closer, I could make out Colorado license plates.

I straightened my jacket and walked down the front steps.

The vehicle pulled to a stop in front of the main entrance, and I got my first clear look at the Warrick family. The driver's door opened first, and a tall man moved around the vehicle, opening the passenger door to help his wife emerge. Flynn Warrick was smaller than I'd expected, with light-brown hair that caught the afternoon sunlight and an intelligent, assessing gaze that took in her surroundings. Even after what must have been a long drive with small children, she looked composed.

The back doors opened, and two small boys burst out with enthusiasm. Twins, both with light hair and bright eyes, began pointing at the snow-covered landscape and chattering excitedly about horses and mountains.

Flynn lifted out an infant carrier. Even from a distance, I could see the tiny face surrounded by soft blankets and small hands that moved restlessly as the baby began to wake.

"Mr. and Mrs. Warrick," I said, approaching them. "I'm Javier Wyatt, owner of Sangre Vista, but please call me JW. Welcome to our ranch."

Her handshake was firm, and her gaze direct. "Thank you for accommodating us. Your property is even more beautiful than the photographs suggested." She turned to her husband. "This is Irish, and please call me Flynn."

"We're honored to have you here for the holidays. I trust your drive went well?"

"Long but uneventful," Irish replied. His handshake was equally firm, and I noted the way his eyes cataloged details—exits, potential threats, the positioning of staff members who were discreetly observing our interaction. "The boys were troopers, especially considering we've been on the road since breakfast."

The twins had gravitated toward their parents' sides, suddenly shy in the presence of a stranger. I knelt to their eye level.

"I heard you mention horses. We have several here at our ranch," I said, keeping my voice gentle.

The bolder of the two stepped forward, chin raised with the confidence that seemed to run in the family. "I'm Paxon. That's Rooker. How many horses?"

"Twenty-six. Would you like to see them while you're visiting us?"

Both boys nodded enthusiastically, their shyness evaporating. Rooker tugged on his mother's coat. "Mama, can we see them now?"

Flynn smiled, the expression transforming her travel-weary face. "After we get settled, sweetheart. JW has prepared a place for us to stay."

"And this must be your youngest," I said as Flynn adjusted the baby carrier, giving me a clear view of the infant, who was now awake and looking around with curiosity.

"This is Rowan," she said. "She's been an angel during the drive."

She was a beautiful child with dark hair that curled softly against her forehead, and eyes that seemed remarkably alert. The infant stirred, her gaze focusing on my face with the intent concentration that babies sometimes displayed when processing new information.

"That's unusual," Irish observed, his tone neutral but his eyes watchful. "She's wary around strangers."

I wasn't sure how to respond to that, so I simply said, "She's beautiful. You're devoted parents." I took a step back to address the whole family. "Shall we get you settled? I think you'll find Pueblo Moon comfortable, and if there's anything at all you need during your stay, please don't hesitate to ask."

As I guided them to their cabin, then helped take their luggage inside, I noted details like how Flynn and Irish moved as a coordinated team, anticipating each other's needs without discussion. How the twins stayed close to their parents but remained curious and engaged with their new environment. How they all seemed delighted by the Christmas decorations we'd arranged throughout the property.

They were a nice family, close-knit and the kind of guests who would appreciate what Sangre Vista had to offer, and the type of people who made this business feel worthwhile rather than merely profitable.

As I left the cabin and turned to the main lodge, I took a deep breath and let it out slowly. This was going to be a memorable month—for all of us.

2

The afternoon of December 23 brought a sense of anticipation I hadn't felt in years. The Warrick family had arrived and settled into Pueblo Moon, their presence transforming the ranch's atmosphere.

As evening approached, I made my way to their cabin. The porch light glowed against the gathering dusk, and through the windows, I could see the family moving about inside—Irish helping the boys out of their winter gear while Flynn tended to the baby.

I knocked, and Irish answered.

"Good evening," I said. "I hope you've had time to settle in."

"We have, thank you," Irish replied. "Everything is perfect. The boys are already planning tomorrow's snow fort construction."

Flynn appeared beside him, the baby now calm in her arms. "Is there anything we need to know about the ranch? Any evening activities or protocols?"

"That's why I'm here." I shifted, feeling the weight of this invitation more than I'd expected. "Rather than having you dine alone in the cabin on your first night, I'd be honored if you'd join me in the main lodge. Chef Alton has prepared something special to welcome you to Sangre Vista."

The couple exchanged one of those quick, wordless conversations that spoke of their close connection. Flynn's eyebrows rose with a question, and Irish gave an imperceptible nod.

"That's very thoughtful," Flynn said. "Are you certain the boys won't be too much disruption? They're excited about being somewhere new, which translates to extra energy."

"I'm looking forward to dining with the whole family," I assured her. "Shall we say seven o'clock? That should give you time to get everyone ready."

"Seven sounds perfect," Irish confirmed.

I returned to the lodge, where the staff was putting the finishing touches on the evening preparations. The main dining room had been arranged with a single, large table near the massive stone fireplace. Warm lighting and fresh greenery created a welcoming atmosphere.

Sarah appeared with high chairs and booster seats. "Where would you like these?"

"Near the parents, but where the boys can see the fire," I directed. "And make sure there's space for them to move around if needed."

Alton emerged from the kitchen, his face flushed from the heat of cooking. "The welcome dinner is ready. Herb-crusted salmon and beef tenderloin for the adults, with simple sides. For the children, I've pre-pared chicken strips and mac and cheese."

"And something for the baby?"

"I have pureed vegetables and fruits standing by, in case the parents need them."

At the designated time, the Warrick family appeared at the lodge's entrance. The twins had been cleaned up and dressed in fresh clothes, though Rooker had a small stain on his shirtsleeve. Flynn wore a burgundy sweater, while Irish had changed into a navy dress shirt. The baby was alert in her carrier, dark eyes tak-ing in the new surroundings.

"This is wonderful," Flynn said as I led them into the dining room.

"Mr. JW!" Paxon exclaimed, running toward the fireplace. "There's a big fire!"

"It is big," I agreed, kneeling to his level. "And it's very hot."

Rooker joined his brother, both boys captivated by the flames. Irish moved to supervise while Flynn settled the baby in the high chair next to the table.

"You've gone to so much trouble," she said, looking around the room.

"It's my pleasure. Sangre Vista exists to create memorable experiences for our guests."

As we took our seats, I watched the family interact. Irish maintained a protective awareness of his surroundings while remaining relaxed with his children. Flynn juggled multiple demands, yet she never seemed frazzled or overwhelmed. The twins, despite their energy, responded to their parents' instructions.

"How long have you owned the ranch?" Flynn asked as the first course was served.

"Several years now," I replied. "I transformed it from a working ranch into the guest operation you see today."

"What made you choose New Mexico?" Irish inquired, cutting food for Paxon while keeping one eye on Rooker.

"The mountains spoke to me," I said, which was true enough. "Once you see these peaks, others seem less impressive."

Flynn glanced toward the windows, where the light of the moon outlined the Sangre de Cristo range. "They are magnificent. Somehow more enchanting than Crested Butte."

"Every range has its own character," I agreed. "These have witnessed centuries of history—Native peoples, Spanish explorers, settlers seeking new lives."

"Like us," Rooker announced, his face serious. "We're exploring."

Irish chuckled. "That's right, buddy. We're adventurers, aren't we?"

Both boys smiled before digging back into their food.

As the meal progressed, I was drawn into the family's easy conversation.

"The boys have been talking nonstop about seeing your stables. They help with ours at home, but they're still too young for riding," said Flynn.

"We have some gentle horses that enjoy meeting children," I said. "Perhaps tomorrow, we could arrange an introduction."

"Yes!" both boys chorused, bouncing in their seats.

"After breakfast," Irish added. "And only if you're well-behaved."

The baby had remained content throughout dinner. Now, as dessert arrived—chocolate tarts for the adults and sugar cookies shaped like stars for the children— she grew fussy.

"She's usually asleep by now," Flynn explained. "The travel and new environment have disrupted her schedule."

Despite her best efforts, the baby's cries began to fill the dining room. Irish stood to help, and I could see the parents' embarrassment at the disruption.

"Why don't you take her back to the cabin?" I suggested. "I'll arrange for dessert to be delivered there, and you can all get settled for the night."

"Are you sure?" Flynn asked, bouncing the agitated baby. "We hate to leave in the middle of dinner."

"Family needs come first," I assured her.

As they gathered their things, the twins protested leaving before they'd finished their cookies, but I arranged for the treats to be wrapped for them to take along.

"Thank you for a wonderful evening," Flynn said as they were leaving the lodge. "The dinner was

incredible, and your hospitality has been beyond anything we expected."

"My pleasure," I replied. "Sleep well, and we'll see
about visiting the horses tomorrow."

After they departed, I remained in the dining
room, watching through the window as their figures
moved along the illuminated path toward Pueblo
Moon. The evening had exceeded my expectations.
The family possessed a warmth and authenticity that
made their company genuinely enjoyable, not merely
an obligation.

Later, as I reviewed the day's events in my office, I
reflected on the questions they'd asked and the observations they'd made. Flynn's comment about the
mountains feeling different struck me as perceptive.
Irish's protective vigilance spoke of a man who took
his family's safety seriously, yet he remained open to
new experiences.

My phone rang with a call from my security lead.

"Evening patrol complete," he reported. "All quiet.
The Warrick family's lights are still on, but everything
appears settled."

"Thank you, Jim. Any weather concerns for tomorrow?"

"Clear skies predicted. Good day for outdoor activities if they're interested."

After hanging up, I walked through the lodge one final time, ensuring everything was secure for the night. The dining room still held the lingering scents of dinner and pine boughs, a pleasant reminder of the evening's success.

Tomorrow was Christmas Eve, with its own traditions and activities. I'd begun planning ways to make the holiday special for our guests, especially for the twins, who seemed to find wonder in everything around them.

December 24 dawned clear and cold. I rose early, as was my habit, and began my rounds.

From my office window, I could see activity at Pueblo Moon—smoke rising from the chimney and movement behind the windows.

Sarah knocked on my door just after eight. "The Warricks called to ask about breakfast arrangements. Should I have it delivered to their cabin, or would they prefer the dining room?"

"I will ask what would make them most comfortable," I responded.

"Also, Lisa wants to confirm the Christmas Eve activities you discussed. *Farolito* making this afternoon, carol singing this evening?"

"Yes, all confirmed. And make sure we have those wooden animals from Tomás ready for tonight's gift exchange." I'd commissioned gifts for the children from a local artisan and anticipated they'd arrive today.

I left the lodge and walked to Pueblo Moon to check on the family's plans for the day. Flynn answered the door.

"Good morning," she said, motioning me inside. "We were just discussing what to do with all this snow."

"Any thoughts on breakfast?" I asked. "Sarah mentioned you'd called."

"The boys are eager to explore, so we thought we might eat in the dining room if that's convenient."

"Of course. See you in thirty minutes?"

"Perfect."

As I turned to leave, Flynn called after me. "JW? Thank you again for last night. It meant more than you know to have that kind of welcome on our first evening."

I smiled, touched by her sincerity. "It was my pleasure. I hope today proves equally memorable."

When the family arrived for breakfast, the twins were vibrating with excitement.

"What's on the agenda?" Flynn asked as their meal was served. "The boys are dying to see those horses you mentioned."

"After you've eaten and had time to digest," I said, "we can visit the stables. Then this afternoon, I thought you might enjoy learning about *farolitos*—the *luminarias* we light on Christmas Eve."

"What are those?" Paxon asked, syrup from his pancakes decorating his chin.

"Special lanterns that help guide the Holy Family to shelter," I explained. "We make them from paper bags, sand, and candles."

"Can we light them?" Rooker wanted to know.

"With supervision," I assured him, earning approving nods from his parents.

The stable visit proved to be everything the twins had hoped for and more. Rick had selected three of our gentlest horses for the introduction, and the boys were enthralled by their size and softness. Even the baby seemed fascinated by the animals, reaching out from

Irish's arms toward the velvet noses that snuffled at her tiny hands.

"They're so big!" Paxon whispered in awe.

"But gentle," I added, steadying him as he stretched to reach higher. "Horses can sense when someone has a kind heart."

Flynn stood nearby, camera in hand, capturing the wonder on her sons' faces. "This is what they needed," she said quietly. "After being cooped up in the car for so long yesterday."

The afternoon's *farolito*-making session took place in the lodge's sunroom, where Lisa had arranged supplies and workstations appropriate for small hands. The twins threw themselves into the project with enthusiasm, though more sand ended up on the floor than in the bags.

"Like this, Mama?" Rooker held up a lumpy bag that bore little resemblance to the demonstration model.

"Perfect," Flynn assured him, helping steady his hands as he scooped sand.

Irish documented the process with videos while managing the baby, who had become more social throughout the day. She babbled and cooed, content to observe the activity around her.

As dusk approached, we lit our creations along the pathways leading to the chapel and around the main lodge. The effect was magical—dozens of flickering lights glowing in the darkness, creating a constellation of warmth against the snow.

"It's amazing," Flynn breathed, standing on the lodge's porch with Rowan bundled in her arms. "I've never seen anything like it."

"In old times," I explained as we watched the lights flicker, "travelers could follow these lights to find shelter and safety. They represented hope and welcome for those far from home."

Flynn glanced at me. "Like us," she said softly.

"Like anyone seeking something new," I agreed.

Christmas Eve dinner surpassed even the previous evening's success. I'd suggested we eat at six rather than seven, which Flynn said she appreciated. Alton had outdone himself with a feast that honored both traditional holiday foods and the children's preferences. The twins behaved well, worn out from their day of adventures, while the baby slept in her carrier beside the table.

As the meal concluded, I retrieved the wooden animals Tomás had crafted—a horse for each twin and a small rattle for the baby, all carved from local pine and polished to silky smoothness.

"For us?" Paxon asked, eyes wide as he examined the detailed carving.

"To remember your Christmas Eve at Sangre Vista," I said.

Flynn's eyes glistened as she watched her sons' delight. "This is too generous. You've done so much."

"Children should have magic at Christmas," I replied.

After the family retired to their cabin, I remained in the lodge. The evening had been everything I hoped—warm, genuine, filled with the kind of joy that made the hospitality business worthwhile.

Christmas Day dawned clear and cold, just like the day before.

The family appeared for breakfast, looking rested and happy, the twins chattering about their wooden animals and asking endless questions about the horses they'd met the day before.

"Santa found us!" Rooker announced as they settled at their table. "He left presents in our cabin!"

"Did he, now?" I feigned surprise. "Even here in New Mexico?"

"Mama said he has *gips*," Paxon explained seriously, earning chuckles from his parents.

"GPS," Irish murmured.

After breakfast, we bundled up for a sleigh ride around the property. Rick had prepared the large sleigh with extra blankets and heating pads, and Kit and Carson stepped proudly in their holiday harnesses, bells jingling with each movement.

The twins were enchanted by the experience, their laughter echoing across the snowy landscape as we glided through groves of aspen and pine. Flynn and Irish sat close together, the baby warm between them.

"This is perfect," she said as we paused at an overlook that offered panoramic views of the Sangre de Cristo range. "Thank you for making this Christmas so special for us."

"My pleasure," I replied, meaning every word.

The remainder of the holiday passed in an easy rhythm—quiet time by the fire while the twins played with their new toys, and gentle conversation that felt more like visiting with old friends than hosting guests.

As evening approached, Flynn lingered on the lodge's porch, looking out at the mountains silhouetted against the twilight sky.

"This place is special," I overheard her say when Irish and the boys joined her. "I wonder when we'll find out why we're here."

"You could always ask," he suggested.

"I don't want to be rude."

He chuckled. "Sweetheart, two days ago, Six-pack told you that the trust's codicil said you had to leave your home right before Christmas and spend a month in New Mexico. You're entitled to ask why."

She murmured her agreement as they left and walked in the direction of Pueblo Moon.

Irish was right, but for now, their reason for being here would remain my burden alone to carry.

3

JW

The morning after Christmas, Cora knocked and entered with my coffee.

"The Warricks seem to be settling in well," she commented, setting the cup she'd graciously brought me on my desk.

"They're a nice family," I agreed. "Easy to host."

"I planned to ask if they'd like housekeeping today."

"Good idea. Although they may prefer to have the day to themselves."

"Javier, about—"

When I raised a brow, she refrained from asking the question I anticipated. I wasn't ready to talk about the family to anyone. Even a staff member who knew me well enough to call me something other than JW.

Around nine, I decided to check on the guests' needs for the day. As I approached the cabin, I could hear the twins' voices carrying across the snow-covered courtyard.

"Mr. JW! Mr. JW!" Paxon called out as he spotted me. The boys were hard at work on what appeared to be an ambitious construction project that had evolved from yesterday's simple fort into an elaborate winter village.

Irish stood on the porch with his coffee, supervising the winter engineering efforts.

"Morning," I called out. "Looks like the architects are busy."

"Morning, Mr. JW!" Rooker called out, waving a mittened hand. "Look what we made!"

"That's quite a structural achievement," I said, admiring their work.

Paxon beamed with pride. "Papa helped with the walls, but we did the towers ourselves."

Flynn emerged from inside with Rowan bundled against her chest. "They've been out here since shortly after sunrise. I hope they didn't wake anyone."

"The staff is always up early, and there are no other guests to disturb."

Flynn's eyes scrunched. "No other guests?"

"That's right. So, how did everyone sleep?" I asked.

"The twins slept like rocks," Irish answered.

"And you?" I directed the question to Flynn, noting the relaxed set of her shoulders compared to their arrival day.

"Better than I expected, being away from home," she admitted. "There's something peaceful about this place."

"The mountains of New Mexico have that effect on people. You'd be amazed at how many times I've heard someone say something similar."

"Is that why you chose this location for your ranch?" she asked, her tone casual, but her eyes attentive.

"Among other reasons," I replied. "Would you like me to arrange any activities for today? The horses are always available for visits, or Lisa has some indoor options if the weather turns."

"Can we see the horses again?" Paxon asked hopefully.

"After lunch," Flynn said. "Let's let JW get on with his day first."

"No hurry," I assured her. "Things are very quiet this week. I'll leave you to your plans, though, and hope to see you all later."

Around noon, Sarah came to see me. "The Warricks called about lunch," she said. "They're asking if they could eat in the lodge's dining room, but they wanted to make sure it wasn't too much trouble."

"Of course not. Tell Alton to prepare something simple but substantial. Growing children and mountain air create serious appetites."

"Already done. He's making grilled cheese and tomato soup, with fruit and cookies for the boys."

"Perfect."

I was waiting when the family arrived. The twins were full of stories about their snow village and plans for expansion. They'd dressed up for the occasion— Paxon in a red sweater and Rooker in blue, both with their hair combed neatly.

"We're going to add a castle tomorrow," Rooker announced as he climbed into his booster seat. "With a drawbridge."

"Ambitious," I commented. "Will there be a moat?"

"What's a moat?" Paxon asked.

Irish explained while Flynn settled the baby in her high chair. Rowan was becoming more social each day, babbling and reaching for objects within her range. Today, she seemed drawn to the silver water pitcher on the table, her small hands opening and closing in its direction.

"She's got good taste," I observed. "That's authentic Navajo silverwork."

"It's beautiful," Flynn said, then hesitated. "You seem so connected to the local culture. Have you lived here all your life?"

The question was innocent enough, but it required navigation. "I came here as a young man. The Southwest gets into your blood if you let it."

"Where are you from originally?" Irish asked.

"Many places." I kept my answer brief, then redirected. "What about you? Have you always lived in Colorado?"

"Born and raised," Flynn replied. "Like you, Irish is from all over. Military family."

"Did you also serve?" I asked Irish.

"Yes."

I smiled inwardly when his evasiveness matched my own.

"That explains the observational skills," I said.

He smiled. "Hard to turn off."

"Understandable. A man's first responsibility is protecting his family."

Something in my tone seemed to resonate with Irish. His eyes met mine, and a moment of understanding passed between us.

After lunch, we made our promised visit to the stables. Rick had prepared special treats—apple slices and sugar cubes—that the boys could offer with supervision.

"They're horsemen," Rick commented to me quietly as we watched Paxon hold out his palm for Fantasma to investigate. "Got gentle hands and no fear."

"Good breeding," I replied, then caught myself. The comment could be interpreted as knowing more about the family's background than a ranch owner should.

If Irish noticed my slip, he didn't show it. He was focused on helping Rooker reach high enough to pat Carson's neck, as the big draft horse lowered his head cooperatively.

Flynn stood nearby with the baby, who seemed mesmerized by the horses' movements. "She loves watching them," Flynn observed. "Maybe she'll be a rider someday."

"We have lots of horses too," said Rooker.

"The mountains are perfect for it," I said. "There's freedom here you can't find in more populated areas."

"Have you always been a horseman?" Flynn asked.

The question touched on memories I rarely shared. "I learned young. Horses were a refuge when things got complicated."

Flynn's expression softened. "They have that quality, don't they? Nonjudgmental, present in the moment."

"Exactly." Most people saw horses as recreational animals or work tools. Flynn understood their deeper value.

The twins played near the stables while their parents relaxed on a bench nearby, the baby content in Flynn's arms. It was a picture of domestic happiness that stirred something in me I'd thought long buried.

"This is exactly what we needed," Flynn said, tilting her face toward the winter sun. "Time to just be together without deadlines or obligations."

"Or chores," Irish added.

"We have plenty if you find yourself missing them," I teased.

He chuckled and held up a hand. "No, thanks. Like my wife, I'm enjoying the time off."

"It's amazing what people rediscover when they're removed from daily pressures—especially when they're in a setting like this."

"Is that what happened to you?" Flynn asked, then looked apologetic. "Sorry, I don't mean to pry."

"It's a fair question. Yes, I suppose it was."

Irish settled beside her. "What did you do before the ranch?"

Another question that required navigation. "Different things. I was searching for the right fit."

"And you found it here?"

"I did." That much was true.

When the twins tired of petting horses and announced they were ready for hot chocolate, we returned to the lodge, where Alton had prepared the treats, complete with marshmallows and whipped cream.

"Best hot chocolate ever," Paxon declared, his upper lip decorated with foam.

"It's the Sangre de Cristos," I said, winking. "Everything tastes better here."

Rooker considered this. "Even vegetables?"

"Especially vegetables," I said, earning groans from both boys and laughter from their parents.

"We should explore some of the area while we're here," Irish suggested.

"I can arrange guided tours if you're interested. Though with the children, shorter excursions might be more practical."

"That would be wonderful," Flynn said. "The boys *love* adventures."

While Irish gathered the twins and their things, Flynn lingered.

"JW, can I ask you something?"

"Of course." I braced myself, especially when she hesitated.

"This ranch—it's more than a business to you, isn't it?" The question was not the one I'd anticipated, but I still chose my words with care.

"Some places become extensions of ourselves. Sangre Vista is my home as much as it is a guest ranch."

"I can sense that. There's a lot of love here."

"Thank you. That means more than you know."

She smiled, then rejoined her family for the walk back to Pueblo Moon.

Later, I sat in my office, thinking about the day's events. Flynn's questions were becoming more personal, though still within reasonable bounds for a curious guest.

Over the following days, we settled into a pleasant routine. The boys discovered sledding on a gentle slope behind the lodge, convinced Irish to help them build a snow maze, and developed an elaborate game involving the horses, which Rick indulged with good humor.

Flynn spent hours with her camera, capturing both family moments and the ranch's winter landscape. She had an eye for composition, finding beauty others might overlook—morning light through icicles, wind patterns in snowdrifts, horses standing in their paddock.

"You're quite a photographer," I commented one afternoon, watching her adjust the settings to capture Rowan's expression as she followed the snowflakes' fall.

"Just a hobby, but there's great subject matter here," she replied.

Irish was excellent company, possessing the kind of steady presence that made conversation easy. While I'd been joking about chores, he helped with ranch tasks when I'd allow it, showing familiarity I'd expected based on their lives at home.

"You seem to enjoy this kind of work," I observed one afternoon as he helped Rick repair a fence section.

"Flynn's family has been ranching for generations. She could probably run this place single-handed if needed. Me? I'm still a little green, as her brothers say."

The comment was casual, but it provided useful insight.

As we approached New Year's Eve, I planned a special celebration for the family. Nothing elaborate—I sensed they valued simplicity over spectacle—but memorable enough to mark the occasion.

Alton prepared another special dinner featuring regional specialties alongside the usual kid-friendly options. I arranged for a small fireworks display that would be visible from the lodge's main room, timed for the twins' earlier bedtime rather than midnight.

"You don't need to go to all this trouble," Flynn protested when I outlined the evening's plans.

"New Year's Eve should be celebrated," I insisted. "Besides, how often do you get to ring in the new year in the Sangre de Cristo mountains?"

"True. The boys will love it."

The festivities exceeded my expectations. The twins were enchanted by the indoor picnic setup I'd arranged in front of the great room's fireplace, complete with blankets and basket service. Rowan remained alert throughout the evening, absorbing the festive atmosphere.

As the fireworks lit up the sky outside the lodge's windows, I watched the family's reactions more than the display itself. The twins pressed their faces to the glass, exclaiming over each burst of color. Flynn and Irish sat close together on the sofa, the baby drowsing in Flynn's arms, both parents smiling at their sons' excitement.

"This has been a perfect few days," Flynn said as the final firework faded. "Thank you for making our holiday so special."

"My pleasure."

"You know, when we first learned about this trip, I wasn't sure what to expect. A month seemed like such a long time to be away from home," said Flynn, pausing at the door.

"And now?" I asked.

"Now, I'm wondering how we'll adjust to leaving. This place has become comfortable. Familiar. I know that probably sounds crazy."

Irish joined her at the door, settling his hand on her shoulder. "We're required to stay until January twenty-third," he said. "Part of the arrangement that brought us here."

I nodded, aware he was fishing for a response. "Well then, we'll have to make sure the rest of your time here is equally memorable."

After they left, I stood alone in the lodge's great room, watching the last traces of smoke from the fireworks drift across the star-filled sky. Three weeks remained of their residency, and the most challenging part of our time together was yet to come.

When I revealed the truth about Flynn's connection to this place, I hoped her emotional investment in being here would make a difficult conversation more meaningful.

For now, I was content to continue providing the hospitality they deserved while observing their family dynamic and preparing for the revelations that lay ahead. The new year would bring new challenges, but also the opportunity to share the secrets I'd carried for far too long.

4

JW

The first week of January brought a comfortable routine. The weather report showed clear skies for the next three days, followed by another winter storm approaching. Nothing severe, but enough snow to keep outdoor activities limited. I made a mental note to suggest indoor alternatives when I saw Flynn and her family later.

By eight-thirty, the guests had arrived at the lodge for breakfast. The twins burst through the entrance with their usual enthusiasm, while Irish followed with Rowan secured in her carrier. Flynn walked beside him, looking more rested than she had since their arrival.

"Good morning," I greeted them as they gathered around the large table near the fireplace. "Sleep well?"

Irish's brow furrowed. "The twins were up at five-thirty, checking to see if more snow had fallen overnight."

"It didn't," Paxon commented, looking up from his inspection of a cinnamon roll.

"Just a dusting," I replied. "But enough to refresh the trails if you'd like to explore today."

The boys cheered while Flynn and Irish exchanged glances.

"I'd be happy to accompany you," I offered. "There's a trail that leads to an overlook with spectacular views. Easy enough for small legs, but interesting for adults too."

"That sounds perfect," Flynn said. "The boys need to burn off energy, and frankly, we need them to."

While we ate, I was drawn into a conversation about their life in Colorado. Flynn described their ranch with obvious affection, while Irish shared stories of learning to work cattle after years in the intelligence field. The twins interjected with their own observations about the horses, the snow, and the vast differences between their home and here.

"Mama misses it," said Rooker, looking up at her.

She shrugged a shoulder. "Honestly, I thought I would more than I do. Don't get me wrong—I miss my brothers and their families. But…" She trailed off, looking embarrassed.

"What is it?" I pressed gently.

She raised her head, and her eyes bored into mine. For the second time, I waited for her direct question. Also for the second time, she didn't ask it.

After the meal, we prepared for the hiking excursion. The twins required substantial bundling—layers of clothing, warm hats, waterproof gloves. Flynn secured Rowan in a specialized carrier that would allow her to accompany us while staying warm.

The trail I'd chosen wound through stands of aspen and pine, climbing toward a rocky outcrop that offered panoramic views of the Sangre de Cristo range.

The twins ran ahead and doubled back along the trail, while Irish kept watch and maintained conversation with Flynn and me.

When we reached the overlook, the twins were awed by the vista stretching before us. Flynn stood at the edge of the safe viewing area, Rowan alert in her arms, both mother and daughter absorbing the landscape.

"It's overwhelming," Flynn said softly. "The scale of it."

"Your first time seeing the Sangre de Cristos?" I asked.

"Yes, but…" She shook her head. This time, I didn't press her to say more.

Irish approached with the twins, who had discovered a patch of snow perfect for making snowballs. "Watch yourselves there, boys. We don't want to start a war we can't finish."

"Can we throw them at Mr. JW?" Rooker asked hopefully.

"Only if Mr. JW agrees to a fair fight," Flynn replied with a laugh.

What followed was an impromptu snowball battle that left all of us laughing and covered in snow. The twins proved accurate for their age, while Flynn juggled Rowan and snowball construction with impressive dexterity.

For thirty minutes, we were a family enjoying a winter afternoon together. The complexity of my role, the weight of revelations yet to come, faded into the background. This was what I'd hoped for—moments of pure joy, unencumbered by the burdens of the past.

On our return, the twins peppered me with questions about wildlife and weather.

"Maybe tomorrow, we could visit a different part of the ranch," I suggested as we approached the main building. "There's an old cabin that might interest you—part of the original homestead."

Flynn's eyes lit with curiosity. "How old?"

"Built in the 1880s. It's been preserved as a historical site. The children might enjoy seeing how families lived back then."

"Educational and fun," Irish observed. "Sounds ideal."

That evening, I called my attorney from my office.

"Flynn has been asking questions," I reported. "She's intuiting connections she shouldn't be able to make. Her instincts are remarkable."

"Perhaps it's time to tell her the truth," said Gregory. The man was my friend as much as my lawyer.

"She's not ready. Neither am I."

"JW, you've been preparing for this conversation for three decades. At what point will you be ready?"

The question hung in the air after I ended the call. Gregory was right—I'd been preparing for years, yet now that the moment approached, I felt increasingly uncertain about how to proceed.

The next morning brought another clear day, perfect for exploring the historical cabin I'd mentioned. The twins were excited about the prospect of seeing an "old house," while Flynn and Irish seemed interested in learning more about the ranch's history.

The cabin sat in a meadow about two miles from the main lodge, accessible by a well-maintained trail that wound through dense forest. Built from local timber and stone, it represented the kind of homestead that had dotted this region in the late 1800s.

"It's smaller than I expected," Flynn observed as we approached the single-room structure.

"Families were tougher back then," I replied, unlocking the heavy wooden door. "Or maybe they just needed less space when survival was the priority."

Inside, the cabin had been preserved with period furnishings—rough-hewn furniture, cast-iron cookware, simple tools for daily living. The twins explored with fascination, touching everything they were allowed to handle.

"This is how people lived?" Paxon asked, examining a hand-carved wooden bowl.

"For many families, yes," I said. "They built what they needed with materials they could find."

Flynn studied a framed photograph hanging on the wall—a sepia-toned image of a family standing in front of the cabin. "Are these the original homesteaders?"

"The Mendoza family," I confirmed. "They worked this land for nearly thirty years before selling it."

She leaned closer to examine the photograph. "The woman looks so young to have all those children."

"Life moved at a different pace then. People married young, started families early."

"And often died young too," Irish added grimly, reading a placard about frontier mortality rates.

As we explored the cabin's single room, I watched Flynn absorb the details—the handmade quilts, the simple furniture, the practical tools for frontier living. She had the same intense focus I'd noticed when she studied the photographs in the lodge, as if she were trying to extract meaning beyond what was visible.

"Were there many homesteads like this in the area?" she asked.

"Dozens. Most are gone now—either collapsed or removed. This one survived because it was built well and later owners chose to preserve it."

"Lucky for us," Flynn said, running her hand along the smooth surface of a wooden table.

The twins had discovered a collection of antique toys in a wooden chest—carved animals, a primitive doll, wooden blocks worn smooth by generations of small hands. Their delight in these simple objects reminded me why I'd wanted to share this place with them.

"Can we take some pictures?" Flynn asked, pulling out her camera.

"Of course."

She photographed the twins with the antique toys, captured Irish examining the cabin's construction, and took several shots of the interior details. But I noticed she also photographed the family portrait on the wall, studying it through her camera lens as if searching for something.

On the walk back to the lodge, Flynn asked more questions about the area's history—the ranch's previous owners, changes in land use, connections to the broader region. Her inquiries were intelligent and persistent, though she maintained a casual tone that suggested simple curiosity rather than a focused investigation.

Irish, I noticed, contributed less to these conversations, but his attention remained sharp.

That afternoon, while the family rested at their cabin, I reviewed the historical documents I'd assembled over the years. Property records, family histories, photographs spanning decades—all organized and preserved. Soon, I would need to share these with Flynn, but not yet.

The number of storms approaching one after the other would likely confine everyone indoors for several days. Perhaps that would provide the right opportunity for deeper conversations, when the isolation would create a natural intimacy for difficult revelations.

My phone rang with a call from Jim, reporting the evening security check.

"All quiet?" I asked.

"Yes, sir. Though I noticed Mrs. Warrick spent considerable time on her phone this afternoon. Long conversation with someone."

"Family, probably. She's been away from home longer than usual."

"Yes, sir."

"We still have two and a half weeks left here," Flynn said when the family joined me for dinner. "Though it feels like we've been here much longer."

"In a good way, I hope."

"Definitely in a good way," Flynn confirmed. "And thank you for today. The historical cabin, the hike yesterday. We all enjoyed it very much."

"It's my pleasure," I replied honestly.

"Still, I want you to know it's appreciated." She paused, considering her next words. "I hope you don't mind me saying this, but you seem like someone who doesn't have much family of your own."

The observation struck closer to home than I was prepared for. "What makes you say that?"

"The way you watch us sometimes. Like you're absorbing what a family looks like, storing up the memories."

"You're very observant."

"Occupational hazard of being the youngest in a large family. You learn to read people's expressions."

Before I could respond, Irish appeared with the children, ready to depart. Flynn squeezed my arm gently before joining her husband and kids for the walk back to Pueblo Moon.

Later, when sleep eluded me, I reflected on Flynn's perceptive words. Her insight into my behavior suggested she was beginning to piece together more than I'd realized. The conversation I'd been avoiding was approaching, whether I was ready or not.

5

JW

The second week of January brought a restlessness I couldn't shake. I spent sleepless nights, my mind churning with the weight of what I needed to tell Flynn. The routine we'd established—breakfast in the lodge, activities with the children, quiet dinners by the fire— felt fragile, like a bubble that would burst the moment I spoke the truth.

Time was running out. We were past the halfway point of their month-long stay, and I could sense Flynn's frustration with my evasions.

Around ten, I saw the family emerge for their morning walk. Even from a distance, I could see the tension in Flynn's shoulders, the way she kept glancing toward the main lodge as if debating whether to approach.

She was working up the courage to confront me directly. I could sense it.

By lunch, my nerves were taut. When the family arrived at the lodge, I picked up on Flynn's distraction.

She participated in the twins' chatter about building snow animals, praised Alton's cooking, and helped Rowan with her baby food, but her attention kept returning to me with that same assessing look.

"The boys want to know if they can help feed the horses this afternoon," Irish said as we finished eating.

"Rick would love the assistance," I replied. "He's always looking for eager helpers."

"Can we, Mama? Please?" Paxon bounced in his seat.

Flynn smiled at her son's enthusiasm, but when she looked at me, her expression turned serious. "I was hoping I could speak with you privately this afternoon when Irish takes the boys to feed the horses."

The moment I'd been dreading and anticipating had arrived. "Of course. My office?"

"That would be perfect."

The rest of lunch passed in a blur of conversation, but underneath the surface, I could feel the approaching storm—not the weather system moving in, but the reckoning that had been building since the day they arrived.

After the family left, I retreated to my office. The leather portfolio sat on my desk like an accusation.

Inside were truths that would transform Flynn's understanding of her past, her family, and her very identity. Was I ready to share them? Did I have a choice?

At three o'clock, Flynn knocked on my office door.

"Come in," I called, rising from behind my desk.

She entered, closing the door behind her. She'd changed from her casual morning clothes into dark jeans and a burgundy sweater that brought out the gold highlights in her hair, and that I remembered her wearing shortly after their arrival here. It felt like so long ago. Her expression was determined but not hostile—a woman seeking answers, not a confrontation.

"Thank you for making time," she said, settling into the chair across from my desk.

"Of course. What's on your mind?"

She folded her hands in her lap, gathering her thoughts. "I've been here over two weeks now, and I keep feeling like there's something I'm missing. Something important."

I waited, letting her speak.

"The trust that brought us here—it's been orchestrating my family's lives for three years. Each of my brothers was sent somewhere different, somewhere connected to our mother's past." Her eyes met mine directly. "This place, this ranch, you—there's a connection, isn't there?"

The question hung in the air between us. I could deflect again, offer another vague non-answer, but Flynn's intelligence and persistence had made that increasingly difficult. Yet I wasn't ready to reveal everything. Not yet.

"What makes you think that?" I asked, curious about her reasoning.

"A dozen small things. The way you look at my children sometimes, like you're seeing someone else in their faces. The photographs in the lodge—several show Colorado landscapes that look familiar. Your questions about our family feel too personal for a stranger making conversation."

"You're very observant," I said.

"That's not an answer."

"No, it's not." I stood and moved to the window, needing distance. "Flynn, there are...complexities to your family's situation that I understand better than most would."

"What does that mean?"

I turned back to face her. "It means your intuition is correct. There are connections I haven't shared."

Her expression shifted from frustration to apprehension. "What kind of connections?"

"The kind that require more time to explain properly." I returned to my desk but remained standing. "Far more than can be covered in a few hours."

Flynn studied my face, weighing whether to push harder or accept the deflection. "You're asking me to be patient."

"I'm asking you to trust that when the time is right, you'll have the answers you're seeking."

"When will that be?"

"Soon."

She stood, her eyes boring into mine. "I'm left with little choice. As we both know, if I leave, our family will lose everything."

The observation stung because it held truth. "I'm sorry, Flynn."

She folded her arms. "You're sorry? For what? Do you realize that me having to be here ripped me away from my family? The kind of holiday I'd longed for all my life. One I finally experienced last year?"

"You're here because someone who cares deeply about your family wanted to ensure we had this time together. This place. These memories."

"Someone who cares about our family." Flynn repeated the words slowly. "You?"

I met her gaze but said nothing.

"I need to go," she said abruptly, moving toward the door. "The boys will be wondering where I am."

At the threshold, she paused without turning around. "This conversation isn't over."

"I know."

"There's more you're not telling me."

"Yes."

"A lot more."

"Yes."

After she left, I stood by the window, watching her figure disappear along the path toward the cabin where her family waited.

I pulled out my phone and sent a text to Jim. *Weather update?*

His response came quickly. *The storm isn't due to arrive as early as expected. Probably forty-eight hours instead of twenty-four.*

Good. The place where I'd hoped to start this conversation wouldn't be as easily accessible if the weather turned. Perhaps we could meet there in the morning. Just the two of us.

The family joined me for dinner that evening, but the atmosphere had shifted. Irish seemed to sense his wife's tension, though he gave no indication of knowing its source. His protective instincts were clearly heightened, his attention shifting frequently between Flynn and me as if trying to read the dynamics of our earlier conversation.

"The weather doesn't look as bad as I'd heard it was going to be," he observed as we finished the main course.

"The forecast shows several inches heading our way, but not until the day after tomorrow," I confirmed.

Irish nodded. "Good. The boys can get one more day of outdoor energy consumption in before they have to be cooped up."

"I have a surprise for them when the snow does come. We set up a playroom in the east wing," I said when it appeared neither twin was paying attention.

"Playroom?" Paxon's head shot up from his plate.

I chuckled. "Yes. There are board games, puzzles, and other toys," I explained.

"Can we see it after dinner?" Rooker asked, bouncing in his seat.

"If your parents don't mind," I replied, glancing at Flynn.

"Not tonight," she said in a tone that was probably meant for me, but its effect on her sons was immediately evident. "I'm sorry," she added. "But let's save it for tomorrow night. Okay? We have something special planned at the cabin tonight."

Irish raised a brow, and Flynn shrugged. "We'll think of something," she leaned closer to him and whispered.

"I might have an idea," I said in a low tone of voice.

While Flynn didn't appear interested, Irish did.

"I can have Lisa meet you there. She and Rick put on a puppet show they might enjoy. Then perhaps a special dessert?"

Flynn nodded, but her smile seemed forced. Throughout the rest of the meal, her eyes never met mine. Even when I returned to the table after speaking with Lisa and Alton about the kids' surprise.

When the family prepared to return to their cabin, I asked Flynn if I could have a word.

"I'll be right there," she told Irish, who nodded and walked over to the fireplace with all three children. She turned to me once they were out of earshot. "I want you to know that I won't stop asking questions. Whatever connection you have to my family, whatever reason we're here—"

"There's a chapel not far from here. Would you like to meet me there tomorrow? It would be best if we met alone."

Her eyes widened. "What time?"

"Talk it over with your husband, and let me know what works best for your family."

She nodded once. "And you'll tell me why I'm here?"

"Yes. There's a lot I need to tell you."

"Good," she said before joining her family for the walk back to Pueblo Moon.

I watched from the lodge's windows until they disappeared into the night, then made my way to my private quarters. The predicted blizzard may be holding off for now, but tomorrow, I'd walk into another kind of storm. One I hoped Flynn and I were able to weather.

6

JW

"Sarah asked me to deliver this to you," Cora said the next morning when she brought my coffee, then handed me an envelope. I opened it and read the short note inside.

I'll be at the chapel at 11 this morning. -F

"You've been expecting this," Cora said after I folded it and stuck it in my pocket.

"Yes."

"Are you ready?" she asked without having any idea how loaded those simple words were.

The question I couldn't answer sat between us. "I've been preparing for this for a very long time," I responded.

Her expression softened. For a moment, I thought she might say more, but instead, she turned and left.

After she was gone, I tried to focus on the ranch business—reviewing the occupancy projections for spring, approving menu changes Alton had suggested, and responding to correspondence that had accumulated over the holidays.

At ten-thirty, I made my way through the main lodge, checking that everything remained in order.

I was about to put on my jacket when the front door opened and Flynn came in.

"I thought we could walk to the chapel together," she said.

"I'd like that."

We set out in silence, our footsteps the only sound. I watched her as we moved along the path. She carried herself with dignity, so different from what I might have expected, based on the updates I'd received over the years. Motherhood and marriage had clearly strengthened her—there was a confidence in her movements that spoke of someone who had found her place in the world.

The chapel sat nestled among the pines, its white adobe walls bright against the dark trees. Morning light caught the stained glass windows, throwing patches of color across the snow. I opened the door, and we stepped inside together.

She made her way toward the altar, running her hand along the smooth wooden pews as she passed. I hung back, letting her get comfortable in the space.

This place had been my mother's refuge when we first came to New Mexico. Where she could hide when the weight of the new identities and old secrets became too much. After she died, I came here to think, to plan, to figure out how to keep the promises I'd made.

Flynn stopped in front of the window where my mother had pressed columbines between the glass. They represented a piece of Colorado she hated to leave behind.

When she turned to face me, we both started talking at once.

"I need to ask you—"

"There's something I should—"

I gestured for her to go ahead. "Please."

She took a deep breath and looked me straight in the eye. "Are you the trustee?"

She didn't need to explain which trust. If I wasn't— if this was all some strange coincidence—I'd be asking what she meant.

But I was. And after thirty years of keeping secrets, she deserved a straight answer. "I am."

She let out a long breath, her shoulders dropping.

"How long have you suspected?" I asked.

"Part of me knew from the day we got here. But I wasn't sure until right now," she said. "The way you looked at me sometimes, like you were seeing someone else. And this gut feeling that you were waiting for us. For me."

"As I said, I have a lot to tell you."

Color rose in my cheeks. I'd gotten used to staying in the shadows, watching from a distance. Standing here with her made me feel exposed in a way I hadn't expected.

She smiled as she pointed at my face.

"You're blushing," she said. "I didn't think that was possible."

I couldn't help but smile back. "I guess I am."

She looked at me differently now, like she was seeing me for the first time. The wall that had gone up between us yesterday came down with my admission. We weren't adversaries, just two people with a complicated history to sort through.

I felt the pressure of everything else I needed to tell her. I'd been planning this conversation for years, rehearsing what I'd say and how I'd explain it all. But now that we were here, I realized no amount of planning could make this easy.

"Shall we sit?" I asked, motioning to the pews.

We settled facing each other, close enough to talk without raising our voices, but with enough space that neither of us felt crowded.

"Why was my stipulation only a month when my brothers each had to commit a full year?" she asked in a voice stronger than I'd anticipated.

"With you, I only needed to confirm that you and Irish were truly happy together. Once I was certain of that, my plan was to tell you everything."

She looked puzzled. "But with my brothers?"

"Each stipulation served a different purpose."

She shook her head. "None of this makes sense. How are you related to my mother? To us?"

"For you to understand, I have to start at the beginning."

"I'm listening."

"Fifty years ago, a young woman named Ursula Marquez was working at a restaurant called the Goat, in East Aurora, New York."

"Right," Flynn said. "I know about the original."

"It was owned by Ursula's parents, Felipe and Ambrosia Marquez. Ursula's siblings—Pilar and Victor—also worked there."

"Victor," she repeated. "Is that Keltie's father?"

"He is."

She pressed her fingers to her temples, then stood and moved to the pressed flowers, tracing the outline of the delicate petals with her finger. "They're from Colorado, aren't they?"

"Yes. Brought here many years ago."

"By you?"

"By someone who loved the mountains there."

She turned to face me, studying my face, searching for something familiar. "How did you know my mother?"

"That's further ahead in our story. First, you need to understand how it all began, before Patricia entered the picture."

The mention of her mother's name made her shiver. The way I said it—with familiarity—told her the relationship had been significant.

"This is…a lot."

"I know."

She looked overwhelmed, and I realized I needed to pace this revelation with care. "Perhaps we should continue tomorrow, when you've had time to absorb this first piece."

"No," she said, turning back to me. "I need to know more. The story you started—about Ursula Marquez. What happened to her?"

"One night while working at the restaurant, Ursula met a man named James D. Rooker Jr.—everyone called him JD. They fell in love and married later that year."

"What does this have to do with my mother? With the trust?"

"Everything. But to understand it, you need to know what happened next. JD and Ursula had twin sons a year later. James D. Rooker III and John William Rooker."

Her eyes widened as she processed the initials. "John William. JW—not Javier Wyatt."

"That's right. People called me Johnny back then."

The realization struck her. "Ursula was your mother."

"Yes."

"And your brother?"

"Jimmy stayed with our father in East Aurora when we left." I couldn't keep the sadness from my voice. "We took different paths."

She reached for the pew, then sat back down. "When you left? You and your mother and…?"

"Your mother. Patricia." The name felt heavy on my tongue. "We all left together."

She stared at me. "You knew my mother."

"We were more like siblings than aunt and nephew."

"Aunt and nephew?" Her voice was barely a whisper.

"Yes, Patricia was my aunt. My father was her brother."

The chapel fell silent except for her sharp intake of breath.

"Your mother was pregnant when we left East Aurora. With Buck. JD—my father—tried to force her to end the pregnancy. My mother and I couldn't stand by and let that happen."

"So you all fled."

"We had help. Someone with resources who cared about Patricia. Someone who arranged for us to disappear."

Her hands were trembling now. "Who?"

"Her name was Cena Covert. She was Patricia's and my father's aunt and had more money and influence than any of us realized. She orchestrated our journey."

I watched her process this, seeing the moment when she understood that her entire family history—everything she'd believed about how her parents met, how they ended up in Colorado—had been orchestrated by forces she never knew existed.

"I know that name. Cord talked about her."

"Yes. It was her estate where he spent his year."

"My mother didn't just happen to end up at our ranch in Colorado."

"No. Cena arranged it. She sent Patricia to stay with someone she trusted."

"Who?"

"Irma Wheaton. Your father's mother."

Her face went white. "My grandmother? She was part of this?"

"Cena and Irma had been friends in college. When Patricia needed somewhere safe to go, Irma agreed to help."

"So my parents meeting…"

"Wasn't chance. Though their feelings for each other were real."

She buried her face in her hands. "Everything was arranged. My mother's entire life was manipulated."

"She was eighteen and pregnant. Alone and scared. The people who cared about her did what they thought was best to protect her."

"Including you."

"Including me."

She looked up at me, tears in her eyes. "How old were you?"

"Eighteen as well. We graduated high school together before we left."

"And you've been watching our family ever since."

"Not the whole time. When your mother was diagnosed with cancer, she made me promise to look after her children. The trust was her idea—a way to ensure you were all taken care of and that you would know your history when the time was right."

She stood again, pacing to the altar. "That's why Cord was sent to East Aurora—to learn about our mother's past."

"Yes, that was part of it."

"But the others...Porter at the Morris Ranch, Holt staying in Crested Butte. Those weren't about her history, were they?"

"No. Some were about learning Patricia's story. Others were about healing, about finding what each of you needed."

"And me? Why here?"

"Because this is where we ended up after leaving Colorado. My mother and I lived in Crested Butte for six years before relocating to New Mexico. This ranch became our home."

She turned to face me, her eyes showing full understanding. "You're not just the trustee. You're my cousin."

"Yes."

"Family."

The word sat between us, loaded with thirty years of separation and secrecy. I'd watched her grow up from a distance, influenced her life through the trust, but hadn't met her until two weeks ago.

"There's still more to tell you—about your parents' marriage, about what happened after we came here, about why Patricia felt the need to create the trust, in the first place."

She wiped tears from her cheeks. "I need some time. To process this."

"Of course."

"But I want to know everything. All of it."

"Tomorrow?"

She nodded. "Tomorrow."

As we prepared to leave the chapel, she paused at the door. "JW—Johnny—why now? Why tell me about yourself after all these years?"

"Your mother said she trusted I'd know the right time to share everything with you."

She reached out and touched my arm. "Thank you for taking care of us. Watching over us. Even when we didn't understand why certain things were happening."

"It's been my honor. Your mother and I were very close."

We returned to the lodge in silence, the truth settling between us. Tomorrow would bring more difficult conversations, but today had been enough. The secret I'd carried for three decades was beginning to unfold, and she—Patricia's youngest daughter—was handling it with the same strength her mother had shown all those years ago.

***

I'd been awake since four-thirty, unable to silence the voices from the past that had been stirred up by yesterday's conversation. By six, I'd given up on sleep and made my way to the kitchen, where Alton was already preparing for the day.

"Storm's coming," he said without looking up from his prep work. "Jim says we'll get hit around noon."

"How are we set for provisions?"

"Good for a week, maybe more. I made sure we had extra of everything before the Warricks arrived." He paused in his chopping. "Should be cozy enough with just the one family here, although they might get stir crazy."

I poured myself coffee from the pot Alton kept brewing. "They're from Colorado—they're used to winter storms."

I returned to my office and waited for Flynn to arrive.

At nine-thirty, a knock interrupted my thoughts.

"JW? It's me," said Flynn.

"Come in."

She entered, unwinding her scarf as she closed the door behind her. She looked more rested than I'd expected, though I didn't doubt her questions had multiplied overnight.

"Good morning," she said. "Irish is keeping the kids occupied while we talk."

"How would you feel about continuing our conversation in the library? It's more comfortable than my office, and we'll have privacy. Also, severe weather is heading our way—should hit around noon. We'll likely be snowed in for several days, so it will be a better place for these conversations than trudging back and forth to the chapel."

"That makes sense. We're used to getting snowed in at home—probably more than you are here." She smiled. "I'm relieved we'll have the uninterrupted time we need."

I led her to one of my favorite rooms in the lodge—a cozy space lined floor to ceiling with books, anchored by two leather armchairs positioned near a stone fireplace. I'd lit the fire earlier, anticipating we'd need the warmth and comfort it provided.

She settled into one of the chairs while I took the other, the portfolio resting on the small table between us.

"Where would you like me to start?" I asked.

"Before we do, you should know I called my brothers last night and told them you were the trustee."

I waited for her to elaborate, and when she didn't, I asked, "What was their reaction?"

She grinned. "Buck said he was heading here immediately."

I smiled too. "And?"

"I told him this was my journey, and if you'd wanted him here for it, the codicil would've said so."

"Good for you, Flynn."

"Thanks." Her cheeks flushed, but her gaze was direct and steady. "Anyway, I know the basics of why my mother had to leave East Aurora, but not any of the details. I'd like to start with that."

I slid a color snapshot of three teenagers standing in front of a small house across the small table between us. Patricia was in the middle, flanked by a younger version of myself and my twin brother, Jimmy.

"This was taken not long before we left," I said.

She studied the image, her finger tracing the edge. "You all look so young."

"We were seventeen years old. Your mother was living with us after our grandparents died. While she and my father were siblings, almost twenty years separated them. He was more like a father figure to her."

"Did you spend a lot of time together?"

"We did. We went to the same school, shared the same friends. Patricia was the best person anyone could know—kind, smart, always looking out for others. That's why what my father planned to force her to do was so heinous."

"The abortion," she whispered.

"When my father discovered Patricia was pregnant, he decided she would terminate the pregnancy. He told her she was going, whether she wanted to or not."

Flynn's hands tightened around the photograph. "How awful."

"Ursula discovered what he was trying to do and paid a visit to Cena. She was my father's employer as well as his aunt. My mom explained the situation, saying she knew people in Colorado and we could go there. Cena agreed to help Ursula and Patricia disappear."

"And you went with them?"

"Patricia and my mother were the most important people in my life. I couldn't let them face an uncertain future alone."

"You said your mother knew people in Colorado?"

"Yes. Victor had moved to Crested Butte for a job. We went to live with him, and while my mom told him she'd left my dad and that I came with her, he never knew about Patricia."

"How did that work?"

"Not long before all this took place, Irma contacted Cena to ask for financial help. Your grandfather had died, and their ranch—the Roaring Fork—was about to go into foreclosure."

Her eyes widened. "Oh my God. So Cena agreed to help them as long as my dad *married* my mom?"

"It wasn't quite that simple, but Cena did hatch a plan. She told Irma that in exchange for bailing them out, they had to take in Patricia and keep her whereabouts secret."

Flynn folded her arms. "So now, you're saying the marriage wasn't part of the deal?"

"Not officially. Irma encouraged Roscoe to get to know Patricia, but he wasn't stupid. My guess is he figured out that her arrival was linked to them being able to save their ranch."

She rested against her chair and stared into the fire.

"We can stop for today if this is too much," I offered.

She shook her head. "No, I want to keep going."

"Of course." I stood and poured two glasses of water from the pitcher I'd asked to be brought in earlier, then began again. "Your mom and I had to be cautious about how often we spoke to each other. Cena made it clear that her top priority was keeping Patricia safe. If my dad found us, she didn't want him to find your mom too."

"Understood," Flynn said, leaning forward. "What happened next?"

"Your parents fell in love. Or so it seemed. I know your mother cared very much for your dad. She would never have agreed to marry him if she hadn't."

"Who knows whether the feelings were mutual," she said under her breath.

"I believe they were. Think about it. After Buck was born, your parents had five more children."

"From what little I've been told about her, she wouldn't have had kids against her will," Flynn commented.

"You're right. She wouldn't have," I agreed.

"I have a question," she said.

"Go ahead."

"My dad adopted Buck, raised him as his own. Was that something Cena forced him to do as well?"

"No. It was something he wanted to do."

When she raised a brow and smirked, I held up both hands.

"We can't know for certain, because they're both gone, but from what your mother told me, he offered."

"From what I heard, he hated Buck."

"There were things that happened that played a part in him developing those feelings."

"What?"

As easy as it would be to skip ahead, I couldn't. For her—and her siblings—to understand how I came to play such an important, albeit secret, role in their lives, I had to tell the story as it happened.

"We'll get to that," I said, which she accepted with a nod.

"Backtracking a little, shortly before your parents were married, Cena purchased the ranch outright and created the Roaring Fork Ranch Trust, something neither Roscoe nor Patricia knew about at the time. If they ever divorced, your mother would retain ownership. Roscoe would get nothing."

"Wow." She sat back in her chair.

"As I said before, Cena did what she thought was best to protect your mom."

"I think that's enough for today."

"I agree."

As she prepared to leave, she paused at the library door. "Does Irish know about any of this?"

"No more than you did."

She nodded, then headed toward Pueblo Moon, where her family waited. I watched her go, thinking about Patricia and how proud she would be of the woman her daughter had become.

The first chapter of our story had been told. Tomorrow, the real work of understanding our family's complicated history would begin.

7

JW

After Flynn left the library the previous afternoon, she'd sent word through Sarah that her family would have a quiet dinner in their cabin. Alton had prepared a basket with simple foods the twins would enjoy, and I'd watched from my office window as Irish carried it along the path to Pueblo Moon. The storm had arrived on schedule, blanketing the ranch in another eight inches of snow, creating the isolation I'd predicted.

I'd spent the evening wondering whether Flynn would return this morning or if yesterday's revelations had been too much to process. The shock of the family secrets, the manipulation by well-meaning adults, and the realization that her entire childhood had been shaped by decisions made before she was born—it was a lot for anyone to absorb.

But at nine-thirty, just like the day before, I heard her knock on my office door.

"Come in."

She entered, looking determined rather than overwhelmed, which relieved me more than I'd expected.

"Good morning," she said. "Irish is taking care of Rowan while the boys compete for who can make the best sculpture from wooden blocks. We have a few hours before he'll need my help."

"Shall we return to the library?"

"Please."

"How are you feeling about everything we discussed yesterday?" I asked when we each took the same seats as the previous day.

She considered the question, hands folded in her lap. "Like I understand my family better and know them less at the same time, if that makes sense."

"It does. There's still a lot more to tell you."

"I know." She met my eyes. "I want to understand what happened after you all arrived in Colorado. How you and your mother built new lives."

I handed Flynn a photo of the exterior of a rustic building with a simple wooden sign. "This was taken about a year after we arrived in Crested Butte."

She studied the image. "The Goat. I've been in it hundreds of times, growing up. Keltie told us that

Victor and Ursula were the original owners. Then they sold it to the Rice family, but bought it back last year."

"A couple of months after we arrived in Colorado, Victor and Ursula decided to sell the original Goat in East Aurora. Pilar had no interest in running it, and their parents died years earlier."

"That must have been hard."

"It was their final break from the old life. But instead of mourning what was gone, Ursula and Victor decided to rebuild what they'd lost. They bought an old saloon that needed work but had good bones. Cena gave them the money for the purchase, and what they got out of the sale of the other place covered the cost of the renovations."

Her expression grew thoughtful. "Weren't you worried that would make it easier for your father to find you?"

"Like she did with Roaring Fork, Cena structured the purchase through an LLC called VMC Enterprises. If my father ever discovered its existence, he might assume it belonged to Victor alone, but he never would've been able to prove it unless he showed up in Colorado."

"What if he had?"

I chuckled. "Cena kept private investigators on salary. Nothing happened that woman didn't know about. If JD or Jimmy left home even for a few minutes, she knew where they'd gone and for how long."

Her eyes widened. "Wow."

"I'd say she was a control freak, but the truth is, she made our lives possible. Not just Patricia's, but mine and my mom's too."

"Did you work there?"

"All three of us did. Victor handled the business side, Ursula managed the kitchen, and I did everything else—bartending, maintenance, whatever was needed. That's when I started going by JW—John Williams— instead of Johnny Rooker. Later, I changed my name again to Javier Wyatt."

"What about your mother?"

"Everyone knew her as Mary Marquez then."

She set the photograph down. "And my mother? How was she adjusting?"

The question brought me back to those early days when Patricia was finding her footing as a newlywed and new mother. "She was doing well. Better than any of us had dared hope."

"You stayed in touch?"

"Your mother sent this letter to me in the spring, about six months after she and Roscoe were married," I said, sliding a yellowed piece of paper across to her.

Her eyes moved across the page, reading her mother's words. "She sounds happy."

"She was. That first year was good for them. Roscoe was patient while she adjusted to married life, Buck was thriving, and she had Irma's support."

"What changed?" Her voice hardened. "Because the man who raised us after she died wasn't patient with anyone."

"Patricia mentioned that Roscoe drank more than she was comfortable with. Not problematic yet, but enough that she noticed. She said it seemed to be his way of dealing with ranch stress."

"Stress? I mean, I guess I can understand that. He was on his own, where my brothers have each other."

"Even with Cena's financial help, it was tough. Bad weather, fluctuating cattle prices, equipment failures—it all added up. Roscoe was working harder than ever to keep the place profitable."

She folded the letter and handed it back. "What about Cena? Did she continue managing things from a distance?"

"She did. And she was good at protecting everyone involved. The official story was that Patricia had gone to live with a cousin of hers in California. Someone who needed help after a family tragedy."

"Did people believe it?"

"Most did. Cena was known for helping family members in need, so it didn't seem unusual. And she made it plain to my father that he shouldn't look for Patricia."

Her eyebrows rose. "How?"

"She told him that if he tried to find her or interfere with her new life, she'd cut him off and fire him from the job he depended on for survival. Cena could be persuasive when she needed to be."

"But she didn't warn him away from looking for you and your mother?"

"No. She said that if she'd forbidden him from searching for us too, he would have known for certain that we were all together. Instead, she told him it was his own fault that his wife and son had left him."

She absorbed this. "Smart. Cruel, but smart."

"Cena was both of those things. She cared about people, but she wasn't above manipulation to achieve her goals."

Next came an image showing a young woman holding a baby in front of the Roaring Fork ranch house. Even from the faded image, it was obvious that Patricia was glowing.

"This was taken the summer after Scarlett Blanche was born. They chose her middle name for Cena's daughter, who'd died in her late teens from leukemia."

She nodded. "I've never seen this picture before." Her thumb traced the edge of the photograph. "It's hard to reconcile this with what I remember growing up."

"Even though it didn't last, your mother experienced genuine joy during those years. She had two children she adored, a stable home, and a husband who was trying to do right by his family."

"And you? How were you doing during this time?"

The question caught me off guard. For years, I'd focused on everyone else's well-being rather than considering my own emotional state.

"I found my place. Working at the Goat gave me purpose, and being near enough to Patricia to know she was safe gave me peace. For the first time since we left East Aurora, I felt like we might make it work."

"Did you miss your brother?"

"Honestly? No. We were twins, but completely different. My mom used to say it was that way from birth."

"Did you ever try to contact him?"

"No. That chapter of my life was closed. It was harder for my mom. Of course she missed him, but she'd made her choice and didn't feel she could go back. Plus, Jimmy was an adult, not a kid."

"Still, I'm sure it was hard for her."

"It was. Cena sent photos once in a while."

Flynn was quiet for a moment, staring in the distance, then turned back to me. "What did Cena think about Jimmy?"

I hesitated, remembering the difficult conversations my mom had had with Cena about my brother's character. "She wasn't optimistic about his future. She said Jimmy had too much of our father in him—the anger, the stubbornness, the tendency toward destructive behavior."

"She thought he'd end up that way too?"

"Worse. She predicted he'd land himself in jail, or worse." The words still stung, despite how true they'd proven. "But as the years went by, I began to understand what she meant. The choices we made after leaving East Aurora defined who we became. I had Patricia and

Ursula to remind me of what was important. Jimmy only had our dad." I sighed. "And, as you know, Cena was right. Jimmy is in prison for attempted murder."

"He would've killed Sam if Cord hadn't shot him."

I shut my eyes. "The months when Cord was in New York were the hardest of my life. So many times I'd wanted to intervene, but I couldn't. I was bound by the terms of the trust and by my promise to your mother."

"I understand," she said, but I wondered if she did or if anyone would.

"Tell me about when Scarlett got sick," she said a few minutes later. "I know she died of leukemia, but what was that time like for my parents?"

I paused, gathering myself before reaching for a shorter letter that lay in the portfolio. "This arrived when Scarlett was about six months old," I said, offering it to her.

She accepted the sheet, and I watched her expression shift as she read. There was fear nestled between each line—a mother's intuition that something was wrong, even when everyone around her insisted otherwise.

"She was scared."

"Patricia knew something wasn't right, but Roscoe kept dismissing her concerns. He told her growing children went through phases and Scarlett would out-grow what turned out to be symptoms." I handed her a photograph of Scarlett looking pale and listless in her mother's arms. "But her instincts were correct. By early spring, Scarlett had developed a fever that wouldn't break."

"Is that when they got the diagnosis?"

"Yes. She convinced Roscoe that they should take the baby to a hospital in Denver. When the doctors told them it was leukemia…" I shook my head. "When she was eventually able to get away long enough to call us, I could barely understand her through the tears."

"What did you do? You couldn't show up at the hospital."

"No, but my mother could. She posed as a volunteer from a local charity that helped families with their other children when they had a sick child requiring extended care."

The next image was taken in a hospital room. Ursula sat beside Scarlett's bed, reading to Buck, who was a little over a year old. He was curled up on my mother's lap, clutching a stuffed animal.

"My dad had no idea who she was?"

"None. As far as he knew, she was just a kind woman who came during the day to help with Buck so he could stay home and keep the ranch running. The two women were careful to maintain the cover story."

Flynn examined the hospital photograph, worry creasing her brow. "How long did this go on?"

"They spent three months watching that beautiful little girl fight for her life while they pretended to be strangers." I rubbed my temples, the memories still heavy. "I've never felt so powerless. I couldn't visit, couldn't hold Patricia when she cried, couldn't do anything but wait for phone calls."

"And Scarlett?"

I met her eyes. "She died in December. She was nine months old."

Flynn wiped tears from her cheeks, taking a moment to compose herself. "How did my parents handle it?"

"Differently. Patricia wanted to talk about Scarlett, to remember her, to keep her memory alive. Roscoe wanted to pretend she'd never existed." I handed her another letter. "This came a week after the funeral."

She absorbed the words, growing more disturbed. "She sounds so alone."

"She was. The drinking that had been concerning before Scarlett's illness, became much worse after her death. Roscoe was constantly angry—explosive outbursts over minor things. A gate left open, a tool out of place, Buck making too much noise."

"Did he hurt them?" she asked, her voice dropping.

"Not physically. But the emotional abuse was constant. He'd disappear for hours, coming home drunk and furious at the world. Patricia bore the double burden of loss and protection."

Flynn folded the letter with shaking hands. "Did she consider leaving?"

"Many times, but then things would get better for a while. So she endured the bad times. One of the things she did was create Scarlett's Hope Children's Charity. The idea came from my mother's cover story. It made her realize there was a need to provide support to families with seriously ill children."

"You said she endured the bad times. What does that mean?"

"For nearly a year. Those months almost broke her spirit—until everything changed." A different image came next—Patricia holding a newborn baby, with

Roscoe standing beside her, smiling. "Porter was born one year after Scarlett died."

Flynn looked at the photo. "My dad looks hopeful."

"The birth of a healthy son seemed to shock Roscoe back to reality. He realized what he was about to lose—not just his wife and Buck, but any chance at the family he'd wanted. He promised her he'd stop drinking and that he'd get help for his anger. They agreed to work on their marriage."

"Did he keep those promises?"

"For several years, yes. The period after Porter's birth brought some of their better times together. But the damage from those dark months after Scarlett's death…" I shook my head. "Some wounds never heal. The pattern was established—when troubles arose, Roscoe turned to alcohol and anger instead of relying on his wife."

I showed her more photos of Patricia with three boys, then four.

"Despite everything, your mom found strength in motherhood. Patricia had this remarkable ability to separate her roles—to give her children the love and stability they needed, even when her marriage was struggling. We maintained our secret contact system throughout this period. She insisted things were manageable between her and Roscoe. They had their difficulties, like any married couple."

She studied the images. "But you were worried."

"Sick with it. I wanted to help, but I was trapped by the same circumstances that had brought us to Colorado initially."

"What do you mean?" she asked.

I reached for a different folder in the portfolio. "When Holt was still a baby, everything changed. Cena's investigators told her my father had figured out we might be in Colorado."

Flynn's eyes widened. "How? Because of the Goat?"

"We don't know for certain."

I handed her an envelope marked "URGENT" in Cena's distinctive handwriting. "This arrived when Holt was just learning to walk. Cena found out that my father had instructed Jimmy to search for us in Colorado and that he was closing in on Crested Butte."

She scanned the letter, alarm spreading across her face. "He was asking questions in Gunnison, showing old photographs of you and your mom." She raised her head. "Did he find you?"

"No, but it was only a matter of time. The valley is a small community—everyone knows everyone. Someone would've eventually recognized us." I leaned forward. "The worst part was realizing what our presence would mean for Patricia."

Her face went pale. "What did you do?"

"The only thing we could. We ran again. Cena had been preparing for this possibility for years. She had resources in place, new identities ready."

"Where did you go?"

"Here. To New Mexico. Cena purchased the property through a shell corporation. It was remote, isolated, perfect for disappearing." I gestured around the library. "What you see now is the result of more than twenty-five years of building a new life, but when we first arrived, it was just raw land and an old ranch house."

"You were forced to leave my mom."

"I made contact before we left. I'll never forget the sound of her voice when I explained why we had to go."

"What did she say?"

"She told me she understood. That she'd known that day might come."

Flynn took a deep breath and let it out slowly. "What happened next?"

"We disappeared. New names, new identities, no contact with anyone from our past lives. Victor and Ursula sold the Goat to the Rice family, and we vanished. As far as anyone in Crested Butte knew, Mary Marquez and her son JW moved away."

"Did Jimmy ever find out you'd been there?"

"He came close. Cena's people reported he'd identified several people who remembered us, but by then, we were long gone."

She stared into the fire, processing everything. "I have another question."

"I'm sure you have many. Ask whatever you'd like, and I'll do my best to answer."

"The Roaring Fork Trust, I don't remember seeing anything in the copy the attorney gave us about my mom owning the ranch and my dad getting nothing if they divorced."

"There were two trusts. The first was the Roaring Fork Ranch Trust. The second, just Roaring Fork."

"I'd ask, but I'm sure you'll tell me we'll get to that part of the story later."

We both smiled. "You're right," I teased.

"You said neither of my parents knew about the original one Cena drew up. Did they ever find out?"

"Yes, your mother did."

"How?"

"About five years into the marriage, she found a letter from Cena to Irma in a desk drawer when she was looking for ranch receipts. It outlined the entire arrangement."

"What did she do? Did she confront Irma?"

"She did, but your grandmother was unapologetic— in her mind, she'd saved the ranch and provided Patricia with a home and security."

Flynn rested against the chair.

"That's enough for today," I said like I had yesterday.

She nodded. "But there's more."

"Much more."

After she left, I remained in the library, surrounded by the photographs and letters that told the story of our fractured family. Tomorrow, I would tell her about the years that led to her mother's death and the creation of the trust that had brought us all together.

But tonight, I would allow myself to feel something I hadn't felt in thirty years—the possibility that all the running, all the hiding, all the painful choices had been worth it. I'd kept my promise, and Patricia's children had found their way in life. They were closer to each other than they'd ever been, and they were happy.

Nothing was ever perfect, but spending time with Flynn had shown me it was close.

8

JW

After I'd spent twenty minutes staring at the same ranch report, Flynn appeared in my office doorway with Rowan strapped to her in the carrier. Outside, brilliant sunshine sparkled off the fresh snow, and I could hear her boys shouting with delight as Irish organized some kind of expedition.

"The roads are clear," she said. "Irish wants to take the boys sledding while the snow is still perfect."

"That sounds like a good plan. Are you ready to continue?"

"Do you mind if I have the baby with me? She isn't much of a bother."

Smiling, I cocked my head. "I would be delighted if she'd join us."

We returned to the library, where I added fresh logs to the fire.

"I keep thinking about what you said yesterday— that you had to leave Colorado when Holt was still a baby. That must have been devastating."

"It was the most difficult decision I'd ever made. Four young children, a marriage hanging by a thread, and I had to abandon Patricia to protect her."

"I can only imagine how hard that must have been. How much time did you have?"

"Within forty-eight hours, everything was set and we were on our way."

"That fast?"

"Yes." I didn't trust myself to say more without being overwhelmed by emotion. While Patricia knew of our departure and how to reach us, there was another I'd had to abandon—someone I could not risk contacting, no matter how much it broke my heart.

I pulled out a faded photograph showing a raw high desert landscape with a single adobe structure in the distance. "This was Sangre Vista Ranch when we arrived. Twenty-two thousand acres of beautiful, isolated wilderness. The only things here were a small ranch house, the chapel, and the rustic cabin I showed you shortly after you arrived."

She studied the image. "It's so desolate."

"That was the point. Cena needed us somewhere my father would never think to look." I handed her a legal document. "She'd purchased the property through a shell corporation two years earlier. When we arrived, we discovered she'd deeded it to us."

"Under new identities?"

"Yes. Javier Wyatt and his mother, Grace, originally from California."

"How old were you?"

"Twenty-five. Old enough to understand what we'd lost, young enough to feel like my whole life was ending." Rubbing my temples, I continued. "I was angry—at my father for forcing us to run and at myself for not being able to protect Patricia better."

"But it wasn't your fault."

"That's what my mother kept telling me. But leaving Patricia behind when she was struggling with Roscoe's drinking, when she had four young children..." The guilt never left.

The next photograph showed my mother and me standing beside construction equipment.

"We poured everything into building something new. The first few years were grueling—learning how different the cattle business was here compared to what we managed in East Aurora, figuring out how to make the land profitable, dealing with the isolation."

"How close is the nearest town?" she asked.

"Thirty miles away. For months at a time, we only saw the supply truck driver and the mail carrier."

I handed her a photograph showing the construction of the main lodge. "I channeled my frustration into building this place. If I couldn't protect your mother, I could at least create something that might help support her someday."

"When did you decide to make it a guest ranch?"

"About three years in. The cattle operation was profitable, but not enough. My mother suggested we could share this place with others while generating the income we'd need." A smile crossed my face. "She said if we were going to be isolated anyway, we might as well get paid for offering others the same experience."

"And then?" Flynn prompted.

I reached for a letter from Patricia, and as she read it, her expression shifted.

"She's announcing my birth."

"The first girl born to your family since Scarlett. Your mother was radiant with joy. After losing her first girl, then having three more boys, she had a daughter again."

Flynn's eyes filled with tears as she reread the letter. "She says I have her eyes."

"You do. The same vivid blue, the same expression when you're concentrating."

She wiped her cheeks. "I wish I remembered her."

"She loved you so much."

The next document was different—clinical, devastating. Flynn's hands shook as she read the diagnosis, dated barely a year after her birth announcement.

"She was so young," Flynn murmured.

"Breast cancer. Aggressive. The doctors weren't optimistic." I had to clear my throat.

"What did you do?"

"I felt powerless. She was facing the fight of her life with a husband who was drinking more than ever and five children who needed her to be strong."

Flynn set down the diagnosis. "There's something else you're not telling me."

"You're right," I said, lowering my gaze. "About six months after her diagnosis, I got an emergency call from her. Roscoe had been on a three-day bender since learning the disease had spread. She was terrified."

Flynn's face went pale. "Terrified of what?"

"That he was going to hurt her or one of you. He'd been raging, breaking things, screaming, passing out, then waking up and starting the cycle again. She'd locked herself and all of you in the master bedroom one night while he tore apart the kitchen. She said she thought he might have a gun."

"Oh my God."

"I left New Mexico immediately and made the drive in record time—four and a half hours. When I pulled up to the ranch, I could hear shouting from inside."

"What did you do?"

"Went around to the back, slipped in through the kitchen door. Then I heard Buck and Porter yelling that they had to get help. By the time I made it to the living room, Roscoe was screaming at your mother. He was about to hit her."

"Where were the boys?"

"Buck and Porter had dragged Cord outside after he jumped between your parents and taken a blow meant for her. That seven-year-old boy had launched himself at his father, trying to protect his mama."

Flynn inhaled sharply. "Dad hit him?"

"He did. Then I got between Roscoe and her just as he was raising his hand to strike her again."

"The two of you fought."

"He was drunk and enraged—stronger than I expected. Roscoe got the better of me." Our gazes locked. "That's when your mother shot him."

She gasped. "She shot my dad?"

"She had to. He was getting the better of me, and I couldn't protect her anymore. The bullet grazed his arm. Painful, but not life-threatening."

"Then Cord came back in."

"He'd heard the gunshot and raced inside, thinking his father might have killed his mother. Instead, he saw her holding the gun, Roscoe on the floor, and me crouched over him, trying to stop the bleeding."

"What did you do?"

"I shouted for her to get Cord out of there." My temples throbbed with the memory. "But for just a moment, Cord and I made eye contact. He saw me."

"How bad was my father hurt?"

"Like I said, it was just a graze. While I bandaged him up, your mother talked to Cord in her bedroom, making him promise never to tell anyone what he'd seen. Roscoe passed out from the blood loss and alcohol. When he came to, the next morning, she was waiting for him."

"With the gun?"

"Yes. Then she told him about the trust, about who owned the ranch. She laid out his options—get help and stop drinking, or lose everything."

Flynn was quiet for a long moment. "Cord kept that secret for over twenty years."

"Your mother made him believe it was all an accident. She was protecting him from having to carry the weight of what happened."

"How long did you stay?"

"Three days. Long enough to make sure Roscoe understood the new rules, to help your mom document everything, and to set up better emergency protocols." I met her eyes. "And to spend time with you."

"With me?"

"You were fourteen months old. Walking, starting to talk. Patricia let me hold you, feed you, read you stories. You called me 'Jo,' the closest you could get to Johnny."

Tears rolled down her cheeks. "I wish I remembered."

"You weren't afraid of me, even though I was a stranger."

The last photograph I showed Flynn was of Patricia holding her, both silhouetted against the sunrise. "She made me promise that if anything happened to her, I'd watch over all of you."

"Even then, she knew."

"The illness was aggressive, the treatments were harsh, and all of you depended on her. This time, my mother was unable to help."

Flynn blinked rapidly, composing herself. "You kept your promise."

"I tried to. Everything that happened afterward—the trust, bringing you all together—I gave her my word."

"She chose well."

We sat in silence as the afternoon light faded outside the library windows.

"There's more, isn't there?"

"Yes, and it's the hardest part."

"Her death."

"And what came before it." I pulled out a thick folder marked with Cena's distinctive handwriting. "Your mother knew the disease was winning, and in the months before she died, she asked me to return to Colorado."

Flynn straightened.

"She wanted to create a new trust. One that would ensure you and your siblings would be taken care of, but more importantly, one that would bring you together and help you understand your family history."

"The trust we've been living under."

"Yes. She had specific ideas about what each of you needed." I handed her a document in Patricia's handwriting. "She wrote this herself—instructions for every child."

Flynn read, her eyes moving across her mother's script. "She says Cord needs to know where he came from. That he carries anger he doesn't understand."

"She was right."

"And Porter. She says he needs to learn that being strong doesn't mean being alone."

Flynn continued reading.

"Buck needs to learn forgiveness. Holt needs to know he's worthy of love." Her voice caught. "She saw us, didn't she?"

"She knew each of you better than you knew yourselves. Even at one year old, she could see your spirit, your determination."

"What does she say about me?"

Flynn found her own section and read silently. Tears began falling before she spoke. "She says I need to learn that my family's love isn't something I have to earn. That I'm enough just as I am." She looked up. "She knew I'd struggle with that?"

"She knew you'd be the one to hold everyone together after she was gone. She worried you'd sacrifice yourself for others."

"That's why my stipulation was only a month."

"Once I confirmed you and Irish were happy, my job was to tell you everything. To help you understand you're part of something bigger, something that began with courage and sacrifice."

Flynn wiped her eyes. "I don't know what to say."

"We spent her final months planning. Cena helped with the legal framework, but this was your mother's vision."

"What was she like during this time?"

"Determined. Even as she got sicker, she never stopped fighting for all of you. Her desperate wish was that you would someday know your family history."

"How long did you have?"

"Less than we hoped. A couple of years. I made one more trip to Colorado…"

"To say goodbye."

"And to promise I'd watch over all of you. She was so weak, but her mind remained sharp."

Flynn was quiet for a moment. "Did she suffer?"

"Not at the end. She died at home, with all of you around her. Roscoe had been sober for months by then."

"When did you start…watching over us?"

"Immediately. Roscoe was trying his best, but raising five children alone and dealing with his grief, the task overwhelmed him. So I became your secret guardian."

Flynn leaned back. "My mother died knowing you'd take care of us."

"She died knowing she'd raised remarkable children who would take care of each other." Our gazes connected once more. "But yes, she took comfort in knowing I'd be watching."

"What was it like for you? All those years of staying hidden?"

"Lonely. My mother helped—she understood the promise I'd made and why it mattered. But watching you all grow up from a distance, wanting to help more, but knowing I couldn't…"

"Until now."

"That's correct. Your mother would be so proud of the people you've become. How you've supported each other, built your own families, found your own paths while staying connected."

We sat in silence for several minutes, the fire casting shadows on the library walls.

"I'll let you decide if you would like to talk about your brothers' codicils," I said.

Rowan woke, and Flynn took her out of the carrier to nurse her. "It isn't necessary. What's next?"

"The years after her death. How I managed the trust. How I decided when each of you was ready and what needed to happen." Standing, I walked to the window, where I could see Irish and the boys returning from their sledding adventure. "But that can wait until tomorrow."

She nodded and stood as well. "Thank you for keeping your promise to her."

"Thank you for making it worth keeping."

9

JW

"Good morning," Flynn said when she appeared at my office door. "The temperature dropped overnight, so Irish is keeping the boys inside today—they're building an elaborate fort in the great room. We have several hours."

"Shall we return to the library?"

"Please."

As we settled into our usual chairs, Flynn seemed more focused than usual.

"I want to understand what happened after my mother died," she said.

I'd known this conversation would come, but I dreaded it, nonetheless. Those years carried pain I'd never shared with anyone.

"From the day your mother passed away, I kept watch over all of you," I began. "Sometimes, from New Mexico. Other times, I came to Colorado."

Her eyes widened. "You were in Colorado?"

"When circumstances warranted it. Your father was struggling—five children, a ranch to manage, and grief that led him back to drinking. Not at the dangerous levels we'd seen before, but concerning enough that I needed to know you were all safe."

"How?"

"I had ways of monitoring the situation." The memories brought back the isolation of those decades. "Your mother had been specific about when I should intervene and when I should remain hidden."

"You never stepped in," she stated rather than asked.

"Buck took on responsibilities no teenager should have to. He became the adult when your father couldn't be. You all protected each other."

Flynn was quiet for several minutes, staring into the fire. "What about the trust? When did you start planning our stipulations?"

"The trust was designed with one crucial element—it wouldn't activate until after Roscoe died. Your mother knew that, as long as he was alive, the household dynamic would remain the same. He was the patriarch, for better or worse."

"So you waited."

"I prepared. Your mom left general instructions about what each of you needed, but people change as they grow. I had to understand who you'd become before I could design the specific requirements that would help you heal."

She turned back to me. "How did you do that without revealing yourself?"

"I had my ways."

The fire crackled between us as she absorbed this.

"That must have been difficult," she said softly.

"It was," I admitted. "But it felt necessary. I made a promise, and I had to keep it."

"What was it like when Dad died? When you finally activated the trust?"

"I was relieved, honestly. The waiting was over. Seventeen years of preparation, and I could finally act."

"That makes sense."

I nodded, grateful she understood. "The trust accomplished what your mother hoped it would."

She stood and moved to the window, looking out at the snow-covered landscape. "There's something I need to say."

I waited, sensing the weight behind her words.

"You've given up everything for us. Decades of your life, carrying secrets, ensuring we were protected." She turned back to me. "When does it end? When do you get to have a life of your own?"

The question struck deeper than I'd expected. "I made a commitment—"

"Which you've fulfilled. My brothers and I are healthy, happy, and connected to each other in ways we might never have achieved without your guidance. The trust worked." Her voice grew stronger. "But my mother wouldn't have wanted you to spend your entire life as a guardian from the shadows."

"Flynn—"

"You've been alone long enough."

The words hung between us, carrying a truth I'd been avoiding. For decades, I'd lived for others. What came after duty?

"I don't know how to be anything else," I said.

"You could learn. With help. With people who care about you." She returned to her chair. "My brothers deserve to know about you. To understand what you've done for us. They're your family too, JW. You're our cousin. You're part of our family, not just its guardian." She leaned forward, her voice gentle but insistent. "This is what she would have wanted," she said. "My mother sacrificed everything to give her children a better life. She wouldn't want you spending yours as an outsider, looking in."

"What are you suggesting?" I asked.

"Come to Colorado with us. Meet your cousins properly. Let them thank you for what you've done." Her eyes lit up. "We're supposed to stay here until January 23. Do we have to? I mean, wouldn't you be the person who would give us permission to leave early, anyway?"

I thought it over for a moment, and she was right, but her suggestion was complicated. "Flynn, I can't just appear—" My resistance was crumbling under the weight of her arguments and my own longing for connection. "What if they resent—"

"They're going to be grateful, not angry. You protected us when we couldn't protect ourselves."

Irish appeared in the doorway with Rowan. "Sorry to interrupt, but someone's hungry."

Flynn stood to take the baby. "Think about it," she said to me. "We don't have to decide right now."

But as I watched her with her daughter, I realized my decision was already made. The isolation that had been necessary for so long now felt like a prison I'd built for myself.

"All right," I said. "I'll come to Colorado."

Flynn's face transformed. "Really?"

"For a visit. To meet them properly."

"That's all I'm asking."

Over the next two days, I prepared for the journey while Flynn made the final arrangements with Irish about traveling with the children.

Flynn called Buck to let him know we were coming earlier than planned and that I would be joining them.

"How did he react?" I asked.

"Curious but welcoming. He suggested putting you up in one of the guest cabins—said it would give you privacy while keeping you close enough for conversations."

"That's thoughtful of him," I said, grateful for the consideration.

I made arrangements for Sangre Vista's management in my absence. The staff was capable, but I'd rarely been away for extended periods. The prospect of leaving made me anxious in ways I hadn't expected—not just about the ranch, but about facing the people who'd been shaped by my decisions from afar.

"Nervous?" Flynn asked as we confirmed our travel plans.

"A little."

She smiled. "They're going to love you."

We departed Sangre Vista early—Flynn's household in their SUV, me following in my truck. The drive to Colorado took most of the day, with stops for the twins and baby Rowan.

As we crossed into Colorado, old memories surfaced from when my mother and I were forced to flee. I was now returning as someone different. The mountains looked the same, but I was changed.

We reached the Roaring Fork Ranch as sunset painted the peaks in gold and crimson. Four figures waited on the main house's porch—men standing together, watching our vehicles navigate the long driveway.

I parked beside Flynn's SUV, my hands tight on the steering wheel. Through the windshield, I could see them: Buck, Porter, Cord, and Holt. My cousins. Patricia's sons.

Flynn emerged first, gathering Paxon and Rooker while Irish handled Rowan's carrier. I remained in my truck for another moment, summoning the courage for what came next.

When I stepped out, the brothers studied me with expressions ranging from curiosity to wariness. Buck, the oldest, moved forward first.

"JW," he said simply.

"Buck." I extended my hand. "It's good to finally meet you."

His handshake was firm, his eyes assessing. "You too."

Porter stepped forward next, offering his hand as well.

Cord hung back slightly, his expression thoughtful but wary.

Holt was the last to approach. "Thank you," he said quietly. "For everything you've done."

The simple gratitude in his voice humbled me.

"Why don't we go inside?" Flynn suggested.

The ranch house looked much the same as it had all those years ago, though warmer now, more lived-in.

"Mr. JW! Mr. JW!" Paxon called out, tugging on my jacket. "Come see our room! We have bunk beds!"

"And horses in our barn!" Rooker added, bouncing with excitement.

"Maybe later, boys," Flynn said gently. "Right now, the grown-ups need to talk."

We gathered in the main living room, where Flynn took charge, arranging chairs in a circle while Irish settled the children with some toys to keep them occupied.

"This is surreal," Porter said as we took our seats.

"It is for me as well," I admitted.

"Before we begin," said Flynn, "As you know, this was my idea. JW's spent decades keeping our mother's secrets, protecting us. I thought it was time he stopped living in the shadows."

The boys—now, men—nodded and murmured their agreement.

"I know you have questions," I began. "About who I am, why I stayed hidden, what I've been doing all these years."

What followed were hours of revelations. Flynn and I took turns recounting the stories she'd learned at Sangre Vista—Patricia and my mother fleeing East Aurora, Cena's protection, the complex circumstances that had shaped their destiny.

We spoke about Patricia's courage in impossible situations. About the night she was forced to defend herself and her children. About the careful planning that went into creating the trust, designed to activate upon their father's death.

The brothers listened with shock, understanding, and occasional anger. When we reached the part about Patricia shooting Roscoe, Cord went pale.

"She made me promise never to tell anyone," he said. "I kept it secret for so many years." His eyes met Buck's, who nodded, giving me the impression that Cord had eventually confided in him at least.

"She was protecting you," I explained. "You were seven years old. She didn't want you carrying that burden."

"But *you* did," Buck observed. "You've carried everyone's secrets."

"As I said to Flynn, it was my honor. Your mother and I grew up together. Protecting her children was the least I could do."

As the evening progressed, I found myself relaxing despite my initial fears. These weren't strangers, judging my choices—they were Patricia's children, carrying her wisdom and compassion.

"I have a question," Holt said as our conversation began to wind down. "What happens now?"

The question I'd been dreading, having no clear answer.

"Now, you decide," Flynn said before I could respond. "Whether you want JW to become part of this family or return to New Mexico alone."

"That's not really a choice," Buck said, turning to me. "You're one of us. People don't get to choose whether they belong."

The acceptance in his response, echoed by his brothers' nods, affected me more than I'd anticipated.

"I'd like to stay for a while," I said. "If you'll have me. There's more to discuss about your mother, about our shared history. And about the trust and what happens next with it."

"We'd like that," Porter said, speaking for all of them.

Flynn stood, gathering her sleepy children. "I think you five should talk without me and the kids."

Before she could continue, I spoke up. "Would you prefer to continue these conversations as a group, or would anyone like to speak one-on-one?"

"We can figure that out," Buck said. "For now, maybe we should just…talk."

Flynn nodded. "I'll leave you to it." She paused at the doorway, Irish beside her with Rowan. "Be nice to him."

10

After Flynn left with Irish and the children, I found myself alone with four men who were strangers but family too.

Buck leaned forward in his chair. "I need to understand something. The codicils—how did you decide what each of us needed?"

The question I'd been anticipating. I'd wrestled with these decisions, never certain I was making the right choices.

"Your mother left general guidance," I began, looking directly at him. "Yours was the one she predicted the closest." I glanced between the others. "Would you like me to speak with each of you individually?"

"Thoughts?" Buck said to his brothers.

"We all know what happened," said Porter. "It isn't like what we were each required to do was a secret."

"Agreed. Start with me," said Buck.

I nodded. "When you left at eighteen, vowing never to return, she worried that even after Roscoe's death, you'd never come back. She died long before you made that vow, but she somehow knew it would happen."

Buck's jaw tightened. "I hated the *sonuvabitch*," he said under his breath.

"Since this was your heritage as much from her as Roscoe, I knew your mother would want you to learn to love it. The only way I could think of to accomplish that was by having you spend time here after he died. That's when I came up with the year-long requirement."

"I hated you for it. Spent that entire year furious at an anonymous trustee who'd stolen my freedom."

"I know. I'm sorry for the anger you had to carry."

"Don't be." Buck's demeanor softened. "That year changed everything. If you hadn't forced me to come home, TJ and I never would have had a chance to build something real together. And I never would have learned to love this place the way I do. Hell, I wouldn't have Buckaroo."

"It would make your mother very happy to hear you feel that way," I said before turning to Porter. "Your situation was more urgent. I'd traveled to Crested Butte, like I did from time to time, checking on all of you. I knew about your struggles with alcohol and had been trying to figure out a way to help you."

Porter's expression grew thoughtful, and he nodded.

"I followed you for a few days, ready to intervene if something happened. I even considered taking your keys away, like I knew Cord did from time to time. But Cord was in New York, fulfilling his stipulation, so he couldn't help." The memory of that night still haunted me. "Then the accident happened."

"You saw it?"

"I couldn't intervene directly, but I watched as you convinced the sheriff to make everyone think you'd been the one driving drunk instead of Maverick. My gut told me the only way for both you and Maverick to heal was for you to spend time at the Morris Ranch."

Porter went still. "How did you know about Cici and Maverick losing their ranch?"

"I learned about it from Aunt Cena," I said, shaking my head with a half smile. "The woman employed a bevy of private investigators. That's how I found out a lot of things. Anyway, I had faith that you would help them save it. You'd already proven your character by protecting Maverick. I believed you'd extend that same protection to Cici."

"So you sent me there."

"I gambled that your compassion would help all of you heal together. I had no idea you'd fall back in love," I said with a wink.

He shuddered but grinned. "Damn, you really were watching me."

"Not just you, all of us," said Holt, shifting in his chair.

I turned to him. "I feared that once you left on tour with CB Rice, it was likely you'd never return to Crested Butte. I also knew there were things none of your siblings knew yet, including about your sister who died. So I made the decision to force you to spend one more year here."

"The charity," Holt said softly.

"As it turned out, you were needed here in a way I could never have predicted. And that led to you discovering Scarlett's Hope—which became Miracles of

Hope—so you understand why everything would go to them if none of you fulfilled the requirements of the trust."

"Because Mom had started it after Scarlett died."

"That's right."

Holt's eyes narrowed. "You were in the hospital cafeteria in Denver, weren't you?"

"Yes," I admitted. "I spent a lot of time at that hospital while Luna went through treatment and recovery. I couldn't reveal myself, but I needed to know she was going to be okay."

"Why?" Holt asked quietly.

"Because you loved her. And because your mother would have wanted me to care about the people her children loved."

Finally, I turned to Cord. "I intentionally left you for last."

Cord's body tensed, and his eyes scrunched. "Why? Because my story is the hardest to talk about?"

"Because your codicil stemmed back to the night Roscoe was shot and what Patricia said to you afterward." I paused, gathering my courage. "Do you remember her words?"

His reply was barely a whisper. "She said that one day, a long, long time from then, she prayed when I learned about the decisions she made, I could understand why and forgive her."

Tears filled my eyes as I looked at him. "Cord, I'm so sorry for what happened to you there. I regretted sending you to East Aurora every single day. I came so close to revealing myself after Joseph Wilkins Jr. attacked you. I spent every day in the hospital's chapel, praying you'd live. Begging Patricia to get God to grant his grace and save you—" My voice broke, and I couldn't go on.

"She delivered," he said, reaching over to cover my hand with his. "I recovered, learned everything about where our mom grew up, who Buck's real father was, *and* I fell in love."

"Which brings up something remarkable," Buck observed. "We all fell in love because of our codicils."

Porter nodded. "Cici saved me in ways I didn't even know I needed saving."

"Keltie, Luna, and Scarlett changed everything for me," Holt added. "Made me realize music was only part of what I wanted in life."

"TJ made me understand what home really meant," said Buck.

"And Juniper…She's my world. I wouldn't have lived without her prayers or her support, either," Cord finished.

I recognized the love in his expression. There'd been a time—long ago—I felt the same depth of feeling.

"Patricia designed the trust to bring you together and help you heal. She never anticipated it would lead you all to find your life partners."

Buck leaned back in his chair. "I don't feel comfortable speaking for everyone, but even though I was livid when that codicil came down, looking back, it transformed my life."

"Same here," Porter said immediately. "That year at Morris Ranch saved my life."

"Me too," Holt agreed. "I thought I was giving up my dreams, but I was actually finding better ones."

"Definitely," Cord confirmed. "The worst experience led to the best outcome."

Their acceptance overwhelmed me. I'd carried the weight of my decisions alone, second-guessing myself constantly, wondering if I was causing more harm than good.

"How long are you planning to stick around?" Buck asked after several seconds of silence.

"I'm not sure."

"I, for one, want to get to know you," Porter said firmly. "The real you, not just the mysterious trustee. And we want you to know us. Our families, our lives."

"The real us," Holt added, "not just what you've observed from a distance."

"You're family," Cord said simply. "That's not something you have to earn or maintain. It just is."

Their words stirred something I'd never acknowledged, and for the first time in decades, I felt like I might actually have a place in this world beyond duty and obligation.

***

The weeks that followed were unlike anything I'd experienced in my life. Instead of watching from afar, I found myself drawn into the daily rhythm of family life at Roaring Fork Ranch.

"You have a natural understanding of ranch economics," Buck said one afternoon as we reviewed the profit projections in his office. "This kind of insight is exactly what we've been missing."

I found satisfaction in contributing my knowledge to something that mattered so deeply to Patricia's children.

One afternoon, while we reviewed cattle rotation schedules, Flynn brought up something that had clearly been on her mind. "JW, watching you work with us on ranch operations has reminded me of something Cord and I have talked about for years. We've always dreamed of turning part of the Roaring Fork into a guest ranch operation." Her eyes lit up with enthusiasm. "Cord's done extensive financial research, and I've studied successful models in other states. Seeing what you've built at Sangre Vista, I was wondering if you'd help us make it happen."

The conversation sparked something in me I hadn't expected—genuine excitement about a new venture rather than just helping maintain the existing operations. Working alongside the siblings on operational improvements and future planning gave me purpose beyond my decades of guardianship, and now, the guest ranch project offered a way to blend my expertise with their vision.

Each of the siblings brought knowledge from their life experiences outside of ranching. Holt contributed insights from learning tour logistics, helping streamline supply chains and improve the communication systems. His creative thinking brought fresh perspectives to problems the Roaring Fork had been tackling the same way for years.

Cord brought his financial expertise to our discussions, showing me portfolio strategies and market trends. His analytical mind reminded me strongly of Patricia—the same careful consideration of options, the same ability to see long-term consequences.

But it wasn't the business discussions that moved me most—it was the ordinary moments. Dinner conversations that stretched for hours, filled with laughter and gentle teasing between siblings. The sound of children's voices echoing through the house as Paxon and Rooker played with their cousins. The way the brothers and Flynn checked on each other without being asked and offered help before it was needed.

Meeting their wives and children added new dimensions to my understanding of who these men had become. TJ's warmth, humor, and the way she anchored Buck while challenging him to grow. I watched her tease him about his perfectionist tendencies and saw how she softened his edges without changing his essential strength.

"You should have seen him when he first came back," TJ told me one evening as we watched Buck teaching the children to play cards. "So rigid, so determined to control everything. It took months for him to remember how to just be human."

"And now?" I asked.

"Now, he knows when to be the boss and when to just be Buck," she said with obvious affection.

Cici's fierce independence and compassion were a perfect complement to Porter's steadiness. I saw how she challenged him to see beyond his own guilt, how her dedication to saving Morris Ranch had shown him what fighting for something truly meant.

"Porter's the strongest person I know," Cici confided during one of our conversations. "Not because he doesn't feel pain, but because he chooses love anyway, every single day."

Juniper's presence felt like destiny. Her family, the Chances, had purchased the original Goat in East Aurora from Victor and Ursula all those years ago when we fled to Colorado. Now, she was married to Cord and running an equine rescue program that embodied the same compassion that had driven my mother and Patricia to protect those who couldn't protect themselves.

Meeting Keltie had been particularly meaningful—she was Victor's daughter, making her my cousin on the Marquez side. Victor had been like a father to me during those years in Crested Butte, and seeing his daughter married to Patricia's son felt like the universe completing some cosmic circle. Even more remarkable, she was now running the Goat—the very restaurant Victor, my mother, and I had built together when we first came to Colorado.

But perhaps the most emotional moment had been seeing Victor himself again. He'd been living in Crested Butte since Luna's illness, and when we came face-to-face, decades of separation melted away in an instant. The man who'd given my mother and me refuge, who'd taught me the restaurant business, who'd been the closest thing to a father I'd known since leaving East Aurora, was there, with tears in his eyes, embracing me like the nephew he thought he'd lost forever.

Our conversations over the following weeks filled in gaps from both our lives. Victor sharing stories of Keltie's childhood and of building his life in New Mexico before eventually returning to Colorado. Me telling him about Sangre Vista, about keeping watch over Patricia's children, and about the promise I'd made to her.

While we saw him occasionally while my mother was still alive, it had been rare, given we lived on opposite sides of the state.

"It's remarkable, isn't it?" I said to Holt one evening as we watched Keltie help Luna with her homework. "You and Keltie finding each other."

"It was like a gift from heaven," he murmured. "She's the best thing that ever happened to me. And when she learned Ursula was your mother, that you and Victor worked together at the Goat…"

"It made everything feel connected," I finished.

The children accepted me with the easy grace of youth. Paxon and Rooker, already comfortable with me from our time at Sangre Vista, served as ambassadors, introducing me to their cousins and vouching for my credentials as a storyteller and horse expert.

"Uncle JW knows everything about horses," Paxon announced to five-year-old Luna during one family dinner. "And Mama makes the best hot chocolate."

"Better than mine?" Keltie asked with mock offense.

"Different," Rooker clarified diplomatically, earning laughter from the adults.

"Uncle JW says if you believe hard enough, anything's possible," three-year-old Buckaroo chimed in with the absolute certainty of childhood.

As the weeks progressed, I found myself integrating into their daily routines. Saturday-morning pancake breakfasts where everyone gathered in the kitchen, contributing to the organized chaos. Sunday-afternoon activities where I learned the family's complicated dynamics and long-standing jokes. Evening story times where I discovered a talent for spinning tales that held the children spellbound.

"You're a natural with kids," Flynn observed one evening after I'd finished a particularly elaborate story about those horses that ran faster than trains.

"I never knew I would be," I admitted.

My growing comfort with openness instead of the decades of secrecy was perhaps the most profound change. For the first time in my adult life, I could speak freely about my thoughts, my feelings, and my past. I didn't have to measure every word, calculate every revelation.

One evening in mid-February, as we gathered for Sunday dinner, I found myself overwhelmed by the scene around the extended table. Three generations of Patricia's family, plus Irish and the other spouses who'd become integral parts of the whole.

"You okay?" Flynn asked quietly, leaning toward me.

I nodded, not trusting my voice. How could I explain that this simple dinner represented everything Patricia had wanted for her children?

"She would have loved this," Flynn continued, reading my thoughts. "All of us together, loud and messy and happy."

"She would have," I agreed.

"Tell us about her," TJ requested. "What was she like as a young woman?"

So I shared stories I'd never told anyone—Patricia's laugh that could light up a room, her fierce protection of those she loved. How she'd defend anyone being picked on at school. How she'd sneak food from our kitchen to give to classmates who didn't have lunch money. How she'd always believed the best of people, even when they let her down.

"She sounds wonderful," Keltie said softly.

"She was, and she would've adored all of you."

Learning about each brother's personal journey and growth became a revelation. Buck's transformation from a CIA operative to loving husband and father. Porter's evolution from guilt-ridden alcoholic to confident partner in the roughstock business. Cord's journey from traumatized child to successful businessman who'd found peace with his past. Holt's growth from restless musician to grounded husband and father who'd discovered that love mattered more than fame.

As February turned to March, discussions began about officially dissolving the trust. The legal framework had served its purpose—bringing the siblings together, revealing family history, and ensuring their financial security. But it was time to transfer ownership directly to them, to remove the last barriers between them and their inheritance.

"It's strange," Cord mused during one of our planning sessions. "For three years, this mysterious trust controlled our lives. Now, it's just paperwork to file."

"Good riddance," muttered Buck.

"Agreed," Porter said. "Though I have to admit the surprises weren't all bad."

"Speak for yourself." Holt laughed. "I still have nightmares about Six-pack's phone calls."

Gregory, my attorney, traveled from New Mexico to handle the legal details. I watched him work with a mixture of satisfaction and melancholy—satisfaction that Patricia's plan had succeeded beyond her wildest dreams, melancholy that this chapter was ending.

"The paperwork is straightforward," Gregory explained as we gathered in Buck's office. "Dissolving the trust entity, transferring all assets to the siblings as equal owners, and ensuring the tax implications are properly managed."

The siblings signed document after document, officially taking control of their inheritance. As each signature was completed, I felt the weight of my guardianship lifting—not disappearing, but transforming into something lighter, warmer.

"It's done," Gregory announced after the final documents were signed. "The Roaring Fork Trust is officially dissolved."

"What are you thinking about?" Flynn asked as the others celebrated.

"Just adjusting," I said. "I've been the trustee for so long, I'm not sure what comes next."

"What comes next is being family," she said simply. "No conditions, no obligations, no hidden agendas. Just family."

"It's that simple?"

"It's that simple. And that complicated. And that wonderful." She smiled.

These people had every right to resent me for the decisions I'd made, the secrets I'd kept, the ways I'd manipulated their lives. Instead, they'd welcomed me with open arms and made me part of something I'd never dared hope for.

***

One evening in early March, Flynn and I sat together on the enclosed porch after dinner, watching the sunset paint the mountains in shades of gold and pink. The children were inside with Irish and the brothers, their laughter drifting through the windows like music. The temperature had finally begun to warm, suggesting that spring might actually arrive in the high country.

"Can I ask you something personal?" Flynn said.

I'd grown comfortable with her questions over the months, but something in her tone suggested this would be different. "Of course."

"Why didn't you ever have a family of your own? In all these decades, you must have had opportunities."

The question I'd hoped to avoid, though I should have known Flynn wouldn't let it go forever. I studied my hands, searching for words that wouldn't reveal too much.

"I suppose I was too focused on other obligations," I said carefully.

"That's not really an answer."

She was right. After months of honesty about everything else, evasion felt wrong. But this particular truth carried pain I'd spent decades trying to bury.

"I loved someone once," I said. "But it wasn't meant to be."

Flynn's demeanor softened. "What happened?"

"Life. Circumstances." I met her eyes, seeing the gentle persistence there.

"Was it someone you had to leave behind?"

Her probing stirred memories I'd worked hard to suppress. Images of dark hair catching the sunlight, bright laughter echoing across mountain meadows, stolen moments that felt like everything and nothing all at once. A love that had to be abandoned when duty

called, when protecting Patricia became more important than my own happiness.

"Yes," I said quietly.

"JW—"

"That's enough for tonight," I said, standing abruptly. "Some stories are better left untold."

"I'm sorry," I heard her say as I walked inside.

"So am I, Flynn."

11

The beginning of July brought the kind of crisp mountain morning that reminded me why I'd fallen in love with Colorado all those years ago. I stood on the porch of the cabin that had become my second home, coffee in hand, watching the sunrise paint the peaks of the Elk Mountains.

Five months had passed since I'd first arrived at Roaring Fork Ranch. What I planned as a brief visit to reveal family secrets had become something I never anticipated—a homecoming to a family I'd never known I could have.

I was amazed at how quickly Flynn and Cord's guest ranch vision had evolved from a dream to a detailed plan during our discussions. They'd done years of preparation—financial projections, market analysis, site selection, operational frameworks—all the groundwork that typically took newcomers months to even realize it was needed. What could have been a lengthy development process was accelerated because they'd already laid the foundation.

But with that belonging came questions I wasn't sure how to answer. Chief among them—what came next?

The trust had been dissolved. Patricia's children were thriving, connected to each other in ways that exceeded even her most optimistic hopes. My promise to her had been fulfilled so completely that sometimes I found myself wondering if she'd somehow orchestrated events from beyond to ensure everything worked out exactly as it had.

Mission accomplished. So why did I feel so unsettled about returning to New Mexico?

"You're up early." Flynn's voice interrupted my thoughts. I turned to see her approaching with Rowan strapped to her chest in the carrier, both twins trailing behind her.

"Old habits," I replied, gesturing toward the sunrise. "The ranch doesn't sleep in, even when I'd like to."

"Uncle JW!" Paxon called out, running ahead of his mother. "Mama says we're going to see fireworks on the mountain!"

"The Independence Day celebration," Flynn explained as Rooker joined his brother at my side. "It's

Crested Butte's biggest event of the year. The whole town turns out."

"I remember from my years living here—the parade down Elk Avenue, food vendors, live music, and fireworks launched from the butte itself."

Flynn studied my face with that assessing look I'd grown familiar with. "You're thinking about leaving before then."

It wasn't a question. I'd been wrestling with the decision for days, and apparently, my internal conflict was more visible than I'd thought.

"I've been away from Sangre Vista for months," I said. "The staff is capable, but it's still my responsibility."

"And?"

"And what?"

"There's more to it than ranch management." Flynn shifted Rowan to a more comfortable position. "You're running."

The observation stung because it held truth. Not from danger this time, but from something equally unsettling—the growing awareness that I was ready for something more than duty and obligation. Something personal.

The memory of our conversation from a few weeks ago surfaced unbidden. I'd walked away abruptly when she pressed me about why I'd never had a family of my own, unable to face the painful memories her questions had stirred. Later, I'd found her and apologized for my rudeness. Her response had stayed with me. "I just wish we could help you find the same kind of happiness you helped all of us find." The words had been echoing in my mind ever since.

"I'm not running," I said. "I'm being practical."

"Uh-huh." Flynn's tone suggested she wasn't buying my explanation. "When did you say you were planning to leave?"

"Tomorrow morning."

"Stay for the Fourth," she immediately said. "It's only three days away. You've been here this long—what's three more days?"

Before I could respond, Irish appeared with a travel mug of coffee, looking like a man who'd been dispatched on a mission. "Morning, JW. Beautiful day."

"Good morning."

"I'm trying to convince him to stay a few more days. Not to leave before the holiday."

"The fireworks are really something," Irish added.

Paxon tugged on my jacket. "Please stay, Uncle JW? We want to watch the fireworks with you."

"And watch Uncle Holt sing on stage after!" added Rooker.

The simple requests from the twins carried more weight than all of Flynn's logical arguments. How could I explain to them that staying meant confronting feelings I'd spent decades avoiding?

"Please?" Paxon said, tugging on one sleeve while Rooker pulled on the other.

I looked at their expectant faces, then at Flynn's knowing smile, and felt my resistance crumble. Three more days. What could it hurt?

"All right," I said. "I'll stay."

The twins cheered while Flynn looked smugly satisfied. "Excellent. You won't regret it."

I wasn't so sure about that, but the decision was made.

The three days that followed passed in a blur of preparation and family activities. The siblings threw themselves into the holiday planning with the same enthusiasm they brought to everything else—multiple conversations about the best spots to watch the parade, debates over which food vendors were essential, and detailed logistics for managing six young children during a day-long celebration, followed by the CB Rice concert, where Holt would be performing with the band.

I found myself drawn into the planning despite my initial reluctance. There was something infectious about their excitement, their obvious love for this particular tradition.

"Crested Butte's celebration is even better than the Big Apple's shindigs," TJ explained as we worked together to pack picnic supplies.

I raised a brow. "That's quite a statement."

"You'll see," she said with a smile. "This family doesn't do anything halfway."

On July 3, the day before the celebration, I walked to the family cemetery on the ranch. It was something I'd been putting off since arriving here, but with my departure now imminent, I couldn't delay any longer.

Patricia's grave was easy to find—a simple granite headstone surrounded by columbines, the flower she'd always loved.

I knelt beside the marker, running my fingers over her name etched in stone. *Patricia Ann Wheaton. Beloved Mother.* The dates seemed impossibly brief for a life that had touched so many people.

"I kept my promise," I said quietly, feeling slightly foolish for talking to granite but needing to say the words aloud. "Your children are happy, Happier than either of us dared hope when we were planning all this, peanut." Funny, I hadn't thought about my childhood nickname for her in so many years.

A gentle breeze stirred the columbines, and for a moment, I could almost imagine her presence beside me.

"Buck found his home again. Porter found peace with himself. Cord learned about forgiveness. Holt discovered what matters most. And Flynn is exactly the woman you knew she'd become. They're all married to people who love them completely, and their children…" I paused, overwhelmed by emotion.

"Your grandchildren would have made you so proud. Buckaroo has Buck's determination and TJ's warmth. Luna is thriving after her battle with leukemia and has Holt wrapped around her little finger. Little Scarlett carries your first daughter's name and has brought such joy to Holt and Keltie. Paxon and Rooker are going to be heartbreakers, and, like her mother, little Rowan has your eyes."

The words came easier now, years of unspoken thoughts finally finding voice.

"They know about you. About us, about what happened in East Aurora, about the sacrifices you made. They understand why you did what you did, and they're grateful for the foundation you gave them."

I stood, brushing dirt from my knees. "Mission accomplished, peanut. Beyond our wildest dreams."

As I walked back to my cabin, I felt something I hadn't experienced in decades—completion. The promise that had driven me for thirty years was finally, truly fulfilled.

But with that completion came an unexpected emptiness. What did a man do when his life's purpose had been achieved?

The next day, we were blessed with perfect weather for outdoor festivities. I'd agreed to meet the family at nine o'clock on Elk Avenue, where they'd claimed a prime spot for watching the parade.

When I arrived, I found controlled chaos. Blankets spread across the sidewalk, folding chairs arranged in neat rows, coolers full of drinks and snacks, and children running in circles with barely contained excitement.

"JW!" Buck called out when he spotted me. "Perfect timing. The parade starts in fifteen minutes."

I found a spot beside Irish, who was keeping careful watch over Paxon and Rooker as they waved small American flags with enthusiasm that threatened to take out anyone within arm's reach.

"They've been up since six," Irish said with the weary tone of a father who'd been managing excited toddlers for hours. "I think they're more wound up about this than Christmas."

"Fireworks!" Paxon announced, apparently feeling this explained everything.

"Boom!" Rooker shouted, throwing his arms wide for emphasis.

The parade itself was exactly how I remembered it—high school marching bands, local businesses on decorated floats, vintage cars carrying town dignitaries, and enough candy thrown to keep every child in the valley hyperactive for weeks.

But watching it with Patricia's family added layers of meaning I hadn't anticipated. This was their community, their tradition. I wasn't just observing a parade—I was participating in something that mattered to people I cared about.

I was in a conversation with Irish and the twins when Flynn's voice interrupted us. "Oh, there's someone I want you to meet," I heard her say.

I turned my head and looked into gray-green eyes that made my chest tight with recognition.

"Maya?" I whispered.

Her eyes widened, one hand moving to cover her mouth in shock. "JW?" she whispered back.

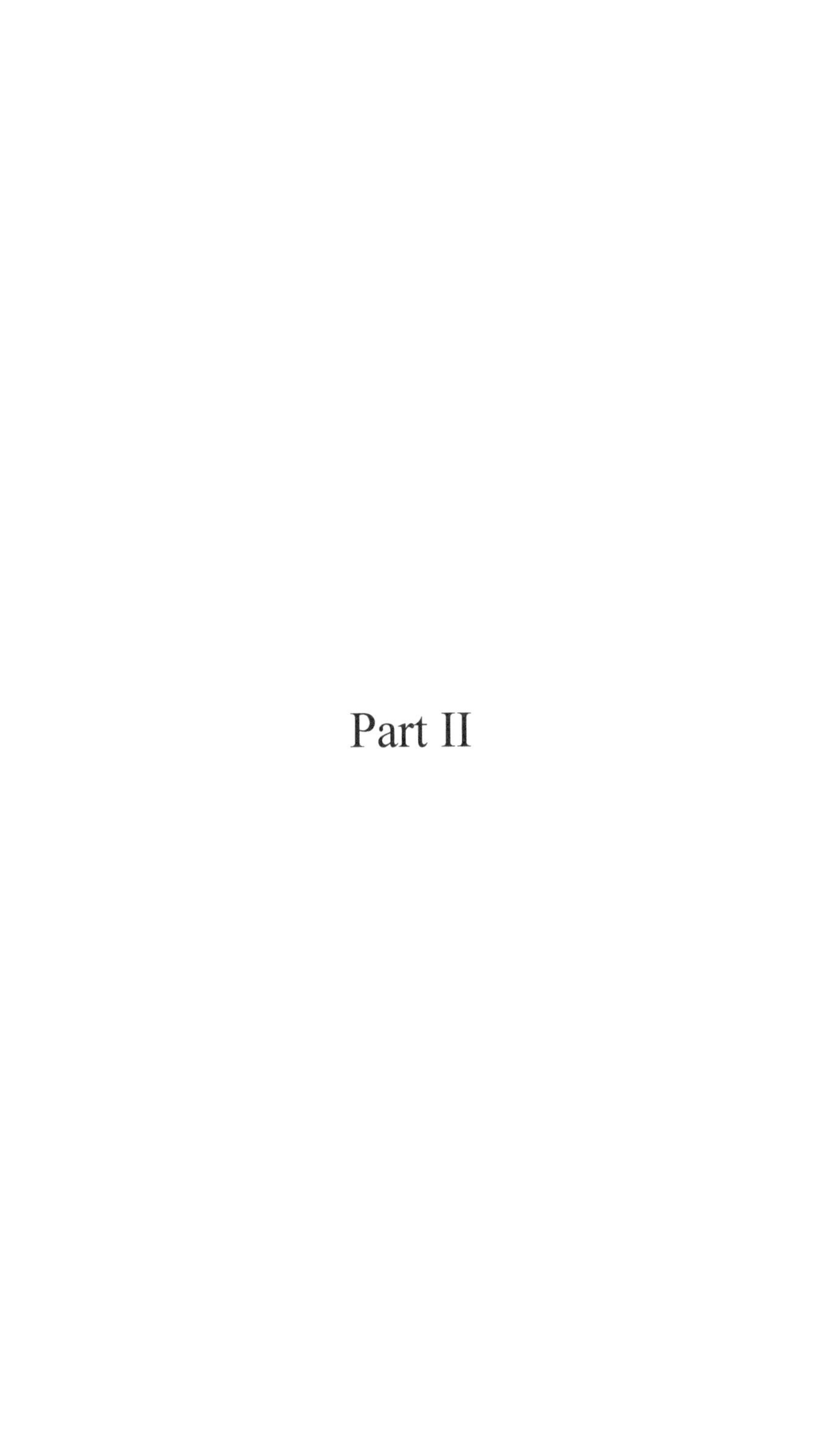

Part II

12

Echo

Those familiar brown eyes met mine, and recognition hit me like a lightning strike.

Nearly three decades since I'd last seen JW's face, and my body knew him instantly—the way his left eyebrow lifted when surprised, the particular intensity of his gaze when processing something unexpected, how his shoulders tensed during internal battles.

"Maya?" he whispered. Hearing the first name I'd stopped using years ago was jarring enough, but spoken from this man's lips sent a shock through my system.

"JW?" I whispered back, my throat constricting.

He looked older, of course. Silver threading through hair that had once been dark brown, lines around those eyes that spoke of decades in the sun and wind. But it was unmistakably him—the man who'd owned my heart completely when I was nineteen, who'd vanished from my life without explanation, leaving me to piece together the wreckage of everything I'd thought we were building together.

Flynn was talking about wanting me to meet some-one—but her words felt distant. All I could focus on was the reality standing before me. JW. Here. In Crested Butte. Looking at me like he'd seen a ghost.

Which, I supposed, he had.

"I—" I started, then stopped. What was there to say? *Hi, remember me? The girl you abandoned without explanation nearly three decades ago? The one whose life you destroyed when you disappeared?*

"Echo, this is JW," Flynn was saying, her voice bright with enthusiasm. "He's been—well, it's com-plicated, but he's family. JW, Echo is the executive director of Miracles of Hope Children's Charity."

Family. The word registered through my shock. JW was family to the Wheatons? How was that even possible?

"We've met," he said carefully, his eyes never leav-ing mine. "A long time ago."

The understatement of the century. *Met.* As if we'd been casual acquaintances instead of two people who'd planned a future together, who'd talked about marriage and children and growing old in these mountains. As if I hadn't given him my whole heart, only to wake up one morning and find him erased from my life.

"Oh!" Flynn's eyebrows rose with interest. "Well, how wonderful that you're reconnecting."

Reconnecting? The word felt hollow. You couldn't reconnect something that had been severed so completely.

I forced myself to breathe, to function, to remember we were standing on the streets of Crested Butte during one of their biggest events of the year. This wasn't the place for the confrontation that I'd stopped envisioning years ago.

"Yes," I managed, my voice sounding strangely normal to my own ears. "It's…quite a surprise."

His eyes searched my face, cataloging changes as I'd been doing with him. The gray in my hair that I'd stopped hiding long ago. The lines around my eyes, some from laughter, but others from tears shed in private. How I held myself differently now—more guarded, more careful.

"Mama! Mama!" A small voice called out, and I turned to see Paxon tugging on Flynn's jacket. "The fire truck is coming!"

"Oh good, sweetheart," Flynn said, but her gaze remained curious as it moved between us. From the corner of my eyes, I could see her filing away details, noting the tension crackling between us, how we couldn't seem to look away from each other despite the obvious discomfort.

As Flynn turned her attention to her children and the approaching fire truck, we stood frozen in our bubble of shock and recognition. The parade continued around us—marching bands, cheering children, rumbling engines—but it all felt muted.

I could see him struggling with what to say, how to bridge the gulf that time and abandonment had created. Part of me wanted to make it easy for him, to pretend that seeing him didn't matter, that I'd moved on completely. But I'd never been good at pretending, and the wound he'd left was still too raw.

"I should go," I finally said, the words rushing out. "I'm meeting friends, and they'll be wondering—"

"Maya, wait—"

But I was already backing away, my pulse hammering. I couldn't do this. Not here, not now, not without time to prepare for whatever discussion we'd have to have. "It was…It's good to see you, JW."

I turned and slipped into the crowd before he could respond, my legs unsteady as I navigated through the groups of families spread across Elk Avenue. Behind me, I could hear Flynn calling to her twins, Irish's deeper voice joining the family chatter, and the normal sounds of people enjoying a holiday celebration.

But for me, nothing about this felt normal.

My friends were gathered near the post office—Misty and Stu from the library, Dr. Cressman from the medical center, and others I'd grown close to over the decades. They were laughing, probably about Stu's annual complaint regarding the parade route blocking his parking spot, but I couldn't join them. Not yet. My smile would be forced, my responses distracted. They'd notice, and I wasn't ready to explain why.

Instead, I found myself walking toward the Slate River, away from the crowds, seeking the quiet I needed to make sense of what had just happened. My feet carried me along familiar paths, past wildflower meadows and aspen groves that had witnessed so many of my private moments over the decades. This was where I'd come to cry when my marriage fell apart. Where I'd walked off the stress of difficult cases at the charity. Where I'd brought my son as a baby when he was colicky and nothing else would soothe him.

JW was here after all this time. Memories came flooding back—ones I'd spent decades trying to bury or at least make peace with. How he'd looked at me during my job interview at the Goat, professional but with an intensity that made my pulse quicken. I'd been nineteen and desperate for work, saving every penny toward some vague dream of college or maybe moving to Denver.

He'd been the one to hire me—JW, who ran the front of the house while Victor handled the business side and Mary managed the kitchen. Everything about him seemed at odds with running a small-town restaurant, like he was capable of much more but had chosen this quiet life deliberately.

During my training shifts, he'd been patient but distant, teaching me the systems while keeping things strictly business. But I'd caught him watching me sometimes when he thought I wasn't looking, and there were moments when our hands would brush while passing plates or reaching for supplies, which sent electricity through me.

It took weeks for him to really talk to me beyond work. The breakthrough came late one evening after we'd closed, when I found him reading a book about ranch management at the bar while doing paperwork.

When I asked about it, he'd looked surprised, then smiled—the first real one I'd seen from him.

"Just trying to learn more about the business," he'd said, looking up at me.

"I grew up around cattle operations in Salida. My dad worked on a few different spreads."

Something in his expression shifted, like I'd surprised him. That was when we really started talking. About ranching, about books, about the mountains and how they changed with the seasons. We talked until dawn, discovering we fit together in ways that seemed unlikely, given how different our backgrounds were.

He'd been twenty-five to my nineteen, and there were things about his past he didn't talk about. I knew he'd come to Crested Butte from back east with his mother, Mary. However, beyond that, he kept his history to himself.

The details had mattered less than how he made me feel—like I was someone special, someone worth listening to, whose dreams and opinions mattered.

We'd spent every free moment together. Long walks along this same river, quiet dinners at his small cabin on the outskirts of town, afternoons where he'd teach me about horses while I told him about my dreams of making a difference in the world. He'd listen, like every word I spoke was important to him. I'd fallen completely, utterly, irrevocably in love with him.

He'd told me he loved me too. The first time was on a night when we'd been caught in a freak storm while hiking. We'd taken shelter in an old mining cabin, sharing body heat under his jacket while we waited for the weather to clear. "I love you, Maya," he'd whispered against my hair, and I'd felt like my heart might burst from happiness.

We'd started making plans. Vague ones at first—maybe I'd move in with him, maybe we'd get a place together.

And then, one morning, he was simply…gone.

I'd waited—God, help me—convinced there had to be an explanation, that he'd contact me when he could. I'd been so sure that what we had was real, that the love I'd seen in his eyes wasn't imagined.

Then came the morning sickness. The missed period I'd tried to ignore. The positive test, showing I was pregnant. With JW's baby. And he was gone without a trace.

In the weeks and months that followed, I kept making excuses for his silence that ranged from reasonable to absurd, telling myself one day soon, he'd return.

But as my body changed and the reality set in, I finally accepted the truth. He wasn't coming back. Whatever had pulled him away was permanent, and I was on my own.

Seeing him today, how he'd looked at me—like I was still someone who mattered to him—stirred up all those old questions. Why had he just vanished? Where had he been all this time? And why was he here now, apparently part of a family I'd come to know through my work with the charity?

I found a quiet spot by the river and sat on a boulder, watching the water flow past while I tried to sort through the chaos in my mind. The sun was warm on my face, and the sound of the water was soothing, but my thoughts remained turbulent. I had so many questions I wondered if I'd ever have the chance to ask.

The afternoon wore on, and I knew I'd have to return to town soon. The parade would be long since over, but the real celebration would continue at the outdoor venue where CB Rice was performing their annual Independence Day concert.

I'd promised Misty I'd meet her there, and I'd been looking forward to it. CB Rice always put on a great show, and there was magic in live music under the Colorado sky on a summer evening. But now, the thought of possibly running into JW again made my stomach churn with anxiety.

Still, I couldn't hide by the river forever. I was a grown woman, not the nineteen-year-old girl who'd been left behind all those decades ago. I'd built a life, a career, raised a son, survived a marriage and divorce, and established myself as someone people could depend on. I was the executive director of a major children's charity, for God's sake. I helped families navigate devastating situations every day.

Surely, I could handle one discussion with my past.

But as I sat and watched the water rush past, I couldn't deny that seeing JW again had shaken something loose inside me that I'd spent decades keeping carefully contained. The delicate equilibrium I'd built my life around felt precarious, as if one wrong move might send everything tumbling down.

Especially when that life included secrets I'd never told anyone about what had happened after he left, about the choices I'd made and the consequences I'd lived with and the realities I'd buried so deep I almost convinced myself they weren't real.

Secrets that, if JW was truly back to stay, might finally demand to be revealed.

13

When the woman I knew as Maya but Flynn had called Echo turned and fled, every instinct screamed at me to follow. But I remained frozen to the sidewalk, watching her disappear into the crowd. The lively chaos of the parade continued around me—marching bands, cheering children, the thunder of vintage fire engines—but it all felt muted, as if I were hearing it through water.

Maya. Here. In Crested Butte. She'd never left. And if she had, she was back.

My hands trembled as I watched her retreating figure weave between families spread across blankets and folding chairs. The same graceful way she'd moved before, though more guarded now. The way she held her shoulders differently, like someone who'd learned to protect herself.

"JW?" Flynn's tone cut through my paralysis. "Are you all right?"

I turned to find her studying my face with sharp concern. Irish had approached from the other direction, Paxon and Rooker flanking him, both boys looking up at me with worry that seemed too mature for their years.

"You look like you've seen a ghost," Flynn continued, her manner gentle but persistent.

In a way, I had. A ghost from a life I'd thought was buried.

"I'm fine," I managed, though my words sounded hollow even to my own ears.

Irish took in the tremor in my hands, the pallor I could feel creeping across my face, and the way I kept glancing in the direction she had gone. He didn't say anything, but his expression held quiet understanding.

"Uncle JW, why are you sad?" Paxon tugged on my jacket, his small face scrunched with worry.

The innocent question nearly undid me. How could I explain to a four-year-old that I just encountered the one person I'd never expected to see again? The one person whose forgiveness I'd never dared hope for?

"I'm not sad, buddy," I said, kneeling to his level and forcing what I hoped was a reassuring smile. "Just surprised to see an old friend."

"That lady was your friend?" Rooker asked, bouncing on his toes.

"She was. A long time ago."

The simple admission felt like ripping open a wound that had never properly healed. Friend. What an inadequate word for what she'd been to me. What she still was, despite everything.

Flynn shared a glance with Irish that said everything. Whatever she'd witnessed between us hadn't looked like a casual reunion between old acquaintances. The tension, the shock, the way we'd both frozen at the sight of each other—none of that spoke to mere friendship.

"Who was she to you?" Flynn's persistence wouldn't be deterred. I knew that.

"Someone I knew before I left for New Mexico," I interrupted, not trusting myself to say more. "We worked together."

The words tasted like ash. Worked together. Another pathetic understatement for a relationship that had shaped every day of my life since, even in her absence.

Flynn's brow rose. "Worked together," she repeated slowly. "At the Goat?"

"Yes."

"And you haven't seen her since you left?"

I shook my head as my gaze returned to the parade's colorful procession down Elk Avenue, but I felt disconnected from the celebration, trapped in a bubble of memory and regret.

Irish stepped closer, his words low enough that the twins couldn't hear. "You need a minute?"

The kindness in his offer nearly broke my composure entirely.

"I need to find her," I said, the admission tumbling out before I could stop it. "I need to tell her, to explain…"

"I'm sure she'll understand," said Flynn, resting her hand on my arm.

Would she? Would anyone? Would Flynn if I told her I'd disappeared on someone I loved without a word of explanation? That I'd made choices that had probably shattered her faith in everything good and decent? That for decades, I'd carried the weight of that abandonment alongside all my other secrets?

Flynn studied my face, and I could see her making the connections. "Oh, JW."

The pity in her tone was almost worse than anger would have been. At least anger would have been deserved.

"I can help you find her," she offered. "I know the town, and she works with the charity we support. I could—"

"No." The word came out sharper than I'd intended. "This is something I have to do myself."

Some wounds couldn't be addressed by proxy. Some apologies required facing the person you'd wronged, no matter how much it hurt.

Irish nodded slowly. "Understood. But if there's anything we can do…"

"Thank you," I said. "Both of you. But this is my responsibility."

Flynn bit her lip, clearly wanting to say more. Finally, the words came tumbling out. "JW, everyone deserves a chance at happiness," she said firmly. "Especially you." I watched as she gathered the twins, explaining that Uncle JW needed to take care of something important, and Irish squeezed my shoulder as they prepared to leave.

"Good luck."

Then they were gone, blending into the crowd, leaving me alone with my racing thoughts.

I started walking in the direction Maya had gone, my feet carrying me away from the parade route and toward the quieter streets that led to the river. She'd always loved the water when we were together. Whenever she was upset or needed to think, she'd seek out the Slate River's banks.

The familiar paths came back to me as if I'd walked them yesterday instead of so long ago. Past the old Victorian houses with their gingerbread trim and wraparound porches. Through the meadow where we'd once picked wildflowers on a lazy Sunday afternoon. Along the trail that wound through aspen groves toward the sound of running water.

Each step brought back memories I'd spent years trying to suppress. Not the circumstances of why I'd left—that burden was already too familiar—but the sweetness of what I'd lost. How she'd curl up against my side when we read together on quiet evenings. The plans we'd made, the dreams we'd shared, the future we'd sketched out in whispered conversations. The way she'd listen as I played guitar and sang silly songs

I'd written about a love that was powerful enough to overcome anything.

All of it was abandoned in a single night.

I'd told myself then that it was the only choice. I couldn't ask her to leave her family and come with me to face an uncertain future. But standing in that crowd, seeing the raw hurt in her eyes as she fled from me, I wondered if I'd been lying to myself all along.

The sound of the river grew louder as I rounded the bend where we used to sit and talk for hours. Sure enough, I found her there, perched on the same boulder.

She looked up as I approached, and I saw her whole body tense. For a moment, I thought she might run again. Instead, she straightened her shoulders and met my gaze directly.

"I wondered if you'd follow me."

Her tone was different now—steadier, more controlled.

"I couldn't lose you again," I said, stopping a few feet away. Close enough to talk, far enough to give her space if she needed it.

"Lose me?" The words came out sharp. "That's rich, coming from you."

The accusation hit its mark, and I felt the familiar burden of guilt settle in my chest. "I—"

"Don't." She held up a hand, stopping me. "I don't want to hear explanations or excuses. It's been too long for that."

"Then what do you want?"

She was quiet, studying my face as if trying to reconcile the man standing before her with the memory she'd carried. The years had changed both of us. Where I saw new lines around her eyes, a wariness that hadn't been there before, I wondered what she saw in me. Gray hair where there had been brown. The weight of secrets and obligations carved into my features.

"I want to know how long you're staying," she finally said.

"Why does it matter?"

"Because I've built a life here. A good life. And I won't have it disrupted by someone who thinks…"

There was steel in her words, a strength that hadn't been there when she was nineteen. Whatever she'd been through in the intervening time had forged her into someone formidable. Someone who wouldn't be abandoned twice. "Thinks what, Maya?"

"It's not important. You found me, but as you can see, there was no reason for you to," she said, starting to rise from the boulder.

"Wait." The desperation in my tone surprised both of us. "I know I don't have the right to ask anything of you. I know I hurt you—"

"Hurt me?" She laughed, but there was no humor in it. "You destroyed me."

I felt my knees nearly buckle and reached for the boulder. I'd known my departure had caused her distress, but hearing it stated so baldly was devastating.

"I'm sorry," I whispered. "So very sorry."

"Sorry doesn't give me back what I lost. Sorry doesn't undo the damage."

The anguish in her words told me there were depths to this conversation I didn't understand. Layers of hurt that went beyond my leaving. What had she lost? What damage had my leaving caused beyond a broken heart?

"I want you to know that it was the hardest thing I've ever done," I said. "If there had been any other way—"

"Are you going to say there wasn't?" She shook her head. "There's always a choice, JW. You made yours."

She was right, and we both knew it. I could have found a way. Could have given her the choice of whether to stay or go. Instead, I'd made the decision for both of us.

"You're right," I said.

The admission seemed to take some of the wind out of her anger.

"Why are you here?" she asked. "In Crested Butte, I mean. Flynn said you were family."

"It's complicated," I said, echoing Flynn's words from the parade. "She visited my ranch."

"Your ranch?"

"In New Mexico."

It was a pathetic summary of the connection Flynn and I had made, but I didn't know how to explain the tangled web of family secrets and obligations that had gotten me to this moment. How could I tell her about Patricia's trust, about the promises I'd made, about finally finding the family I'd never known I could have?

"So you're successful now," she observed. "Own a ranch, part of a prominent family's life."

"I've been fortunate."

"Good. That's good." But her words suggested it wasn't good at all.

The silence stretched between us, heavy with all the things we weren't saying. The river flowed past, indifferent to human suffering, carrying away the detritus of broken dreams and lost chances.

I found myself studying her face, cataloging the changes time had wrought. She was still beautiful—more so, perhaps, with the added depth that came with every trip around the sun. But there was a guardedness in her expression that hadn't been there before. A careful distance that spoke of walls built to protect against further hurt.

"I should go. I promised friends I'd meet them at the concert."

She stood, and I felt panic rise in my chest. This couldn't be how it ended. Not again.

"Can I see you again?" The question escaped before I could stop it.

She paused, her back to me. "This is a small town, JW. We'll probably run into each other whether we want to or not."

"That's not what I meant."

"I know what you meant." She turned to face me. "But I can't do this. I can't pretend that seeing you doesn't bring back everything I've spent so long trying to forget."

Her words hurt. Everything she was trying to forget—our relationship, our love. Reduced to painful memories she wanted to escape.

"Please, Maya—"

"I stopped using that name after you left. I go by Echo now, and I made a new life for myself. Responsibilities. People who depend on me." She started to walk away, then paused and looked back at me. "For what it's worth, I'm glad you found the Wheatons. They're good people."

The kindness in her words spoke of a generosity of spirit that I'd forfeited any right to expect.

I sat on the boulder where she'd been, trying to process everything she'd said. Whatever she meant by saying I'd destroyed her, it was clear that my departure had consequences.

But beneath the guilt was something else—hope. For so long, I'd carried the weight of protecting those who needed me while losing the woman I loved. But those obligations were fulfilled now. For the first time in my adult life, I was free to choose what I wanted.

And I wanted her. I'd never stopped wanting her.

The sun was beginning its descent toward the western peaks when I finally rose from the boulder and started the walk back toward town. Instead of heading to the concert where Maya—Echo—said she was going, I walked toward the Goat.

I pushed through the door, barely able to get inside, and spotted Keltie behind the bar, moving frantically between customers while calling orders to the kitchen. Her usual staff looked overwhelmed, and I could see the stress on her face even from across the room.

"Keltie," I called out, making my way through the crowd. "Need a hand?"

Her face lit up with relief when she saw me. "JW! Thank God. We're absolutely slammed, and two of my servers called in sick."

"Put me to work," I said, already moving behind the bar.

"Bless you," she said, handing me an apron. "Can you handle things here while I check on the kitchen?"

I nodded, falling into the rhythm I remembered from decades ago. Pour the beer, mix the cocktails, take the orders, keep the customers happy. My hands moved automatically, muscle memory from a time when this place had been my second home.

It was while I was pulling a draft beer that I noticed her.

Maya sat alone in a corner booth in the very back, a glass of wine in front of her, staring out the window at the street beyond. She'd changed from her parade clothes into jeans and a blue sweater, and she sat hunched slightly forward, as if she didn't want to be noticed.

My hands stilled on the beer tap. She'd said she was meeting friends at the concert. What was she doing here, alone?

"You okay?" asked the customer waiting for his drink.

"Sorry," I said, finishing the pour and sliding it across the bar. But my attention kept drifting to the back table.

She looked lost in thought, occasionally taking small sips of her wine, but mostly just sitting there, as if she couldn't decide whether to stay or go. Every few minutes, she'd glance toward the door, then out the window again.

The dinner rush continued around us, but I kept stealing glances at her whenever I could. She seemed as reluctant to leave as I was to approach her.

After an hour of steady work, the crowd began to thin. Keltie returned to the bar, looking grateful but exhausted.

"You're a lifesaver," she said, taking over from me. "I don't know how we would have managed without you."

"Anytime," I said, untying my apron. "You know that."

As I prepared to leave, I glanced once more toward Maya's table. She was still there, still alone, still staring out the window. Without really thinking about it, I walked to the bar and ordered a glass of whatever wine she was drinking.

"For the lady in the corner booth," I told the server.

The young woman nodded and took the glass from the bar. When she approached, Maya glanced around the restaurant. Her gaze found mine for just a moment before I looked away, pretending to be busy cleaning glasses.

When I looked back, she was holding the wineglass, and there was the faintest hint of a smile on her lips.

It wasn't much. But it was something.

I left the Goat and stepped into the warm evening air, my heart pounding with the knowledge that everything had changed. She might not be ready to forgive me. She might never be ready.

But for the first time in decades, I had hope that maybe, just maybe, it wasn't too late for us to find our way back to each other.

14

Echo

I stared at the entrance to the outdoor venue where CB Rice's concert was already underway, watching couples and families stream toward the music and laughter echoing across the field. My friends would be there, somewhere in the crowd, wondering why I hadn't shown up as promised. Misty had been looking forward to this all week, had even bought matching T-shirts for our group.

But I couldn't make myself walk through those gates. Not tonight. Not when I'd be terrible company, distracted and raw from seeing JW again. Better to disappoint them with my absence than inflict my emotional chaos on what should be a celebration.

Instead, my feet carried me toward the Goat.

The irony wasn't lost on me—seeking refuge in the one place that held the most painful memories. I'd tried to avoid this restaurant over the years, finding excuses to eat elsewhere when friends suggested it, choosing other venues for meetings when I could. But tonight, the thought of being alone in my house with nothing but my spiraling thoughts felt worse than facing ghosts.

The restaurant was packed, busier than I'd seen it in months. I slipped inside and managed to claim the last empty booth in the back corner, the same spot where JW and I used to sit during my breaks all those years ago. The server, a young woman I didn't recognize, looked frazzled but took my order for a glass of wine with a hurried smile.

As she walked away, I took in the familiar space. The exposed brick walls, the photographs of Crested Butte's mining days, the old wooden floors that creaked in all the same places. Victor and Mary had transformed this place from a run-down saloon into something warm and welcoming decades ago. After they sold it to the Rice family, it had maintained that same character through the years. Now that Victor had bought it back and his daughter, Keltie, was running it, she'd added her own touches—fresh flowers on every table, local artwork on the walls, a sense of community that made everyone feel at home.

But underneath all those layers of renovation and care, I could still see it as it had been during those magical months when JW and I worked here together.

When closing time meant the beginning of our real day, not the end.

My wine arrived, and I took a sip, letting the memories I'd spent so long suppressing surface at last.

After the last customer left and the kitchen was clean, after Victor had counted the till and Mary had finished her inventory, after the other servers had said their good nights, JW would lock the front door and flip the sign to closed. Then he'd walk to the old jukebox in the corner and feed it quarters, scrolling through the selections until he found something perfect.

Usually, it was country music. George Strait or Garth Brooks or some of the oldies like Patsy Cline. Songs that spoke of love and heartbreak and dreams, melodies that seemed to understand the bittersweet nature of small-town life.

"Dance with me," he'd say, extending his hand with that smile that made my stomach flip.

And I would. Every time.

The creaky wood plank floors had been perfect for dancing, smooth from decades of wear, but with just enough grip that we wouldn't slip. JW would pull me into his arms, and we'd two-step across the empty restaurant, spinning between tables and chairs, laughing when one of us missed a beat or stepped on the other's feet.

He had an amazing singing voice that, back then, he swore only I'd ever heard. His breath would be warm against my ear when he pulled me close during the slower songs. Sometimes, he'd change the lyrics, making them silly or personal, until I was laughing so hard I could barely keep dancing.

But when a truly slow song came on—something soft and romantic—the laughter would fade. He'd hold me closer, one hand pressed against the small of my back and the other cradling my fingers against his chest. I could feel his heartbeat, strong and steady beneath my palm.

Those were the moments when he'd kiss me. Soft at first, tentative, like he was afraid I might pull away. Then deeper when I responded, my arms winding around his neck, pulling him closer. The restaurant would disappear around us, the world narrowing to just the two of us and the certainty that this was where we belonged.

I took another sip, the memory so vivid I could almost hear the music, almost feel his arms around me.

The first time we made love had been after one of those dancing sessions. A slow Tuesday night in early winter, snow falling outside the windows, the restaurant warm and intimate in the glow of the Edison bulbs. We'd been dancing to something soft and sweet, maybe "Tennessee Waltz," when the music ended, and we didn't step apart.

"Maya," he'd whispered, my name like a prayer on his lips.

I'd known what he was asking without words. Had known what my answer would be before he even looked at me with those questioning eyes. We'd been building toward this moment for weeks, the attraction between us growing stronger every day, held in check only by his obvious respect for my inexperience and our working relationship.

"Yes," I'd whispered back.

He'd taken my hand and led me to his small cabin on the outskirts of town, a cozy place with a stone fireplace and windows that looked out at the mountains. We'd made love slowly, tenderly, with a reverence that made me feel precious in ways I'd never imagined possible. Afterward, I'd lain in his arms, feeling safe and cherished.

"I want this forever," I'd told him in the darkness, my face pressed against his chest.

"Forever," he'd agreed, his arms tightening around me. "You and me, Maya."

Forever had lasted three more months.

Then, without warning or explanation, he was gone. Not just from the restaurant, not just from my life, but from Crested Butte entirely. As if he'd never existed at all.

I forced myself back to the present, blinking away the sting of tears. My wine tasted bitter now, the memories too sharp, too real. This was exactly what I'd been trying to avoid. Every shadow in this place held ghosts, every creak whispered of what we'd lost.

A flash of movement near the bar caught my attention, and I looked up to see JW emerging from the kitchen, tying an apron around his waist. My breath stuttered. I'd been so lost in the past that I hadn't even noticed him come in.

He moved behind the bar with the same easy confidence I remembered, pulling beer taps and mixing drinks like he'd never left. Keltie's earlier expression of being overwhelmed shifted to relief as the two laughed and joked in the midst of the chaos.

I should leave. Finish my drink and walk out before he noticed me sitting here. But I couldn't stop watching him work, the ways he'd changed, and the ways he'd stayed the same.

He was still strikingly attractive, though silver now threaded through the dark hair I remembered running my fingers through. His body looked strong and capable, the kind of fitness that came from physical work rather than gyms. When he reached for bottles on the top shelf, his shirt pulled tight across shoulders that seemed broader than I remembered.

The years had been kind to him. Whatever life he'd built after leaving here had agreed with him, and I wondered about the details I'd never know. Where he'd gone, what he'd done, whether he'd found someone else to dance with in empty restaurants.

He looked up from the beer he was pouring, and for a moment, our eyes met across the crowded room. I averted my gaze quickly, warmth flooding my face, but not before I saw recognition flicker in his expression.

I forced myself to focus on my drink, on the conversation at the table next to mine, on anything except the way my heartbeat had changed when our eyes connected. This was what I'd told him I couldn't do. I couldn't pretend his presence didn't affect me, couldn't act like seeing him didn't bring back emotions I'd worked so hard to forget.

But, God, help me, I couldn't stop stealing looks in his direction. Every few minutes, I'd risk another peek.

As I stared out the window, my mind drifted again. Remembering how it felt when his naked body pressed against mine. Heat that had nothing to do with the alcohol coursed through me.

I'd loved making love with him. Loved the way he touched me like I was precious, the way he'd learned my body with patient exploration until he knew how to make me gasp and arch beneath him. We'd been so good together, so perfectly matched in desire and tenderness.

My eyes opened wide, and I reached for the glass of ice water that had materialized on my table when I wasn't paying attention. I had to stop this. Whatever we'd had was in the past, buried so deep it should stay dead.

A server appeared at my elbow with another glass, and I looked up in surprise.

"From the gentleman at the bar," she said with a smile. "He said it's on the house."

I glanced toward the bar, and my eyes met JW's. Without thinking, I smiled—just a small curve of my lips, nothing more than courtesy. But his whole face seemed to brighten in response, and warmth spread through my chest that I could not afford to feel.

I looked away quickly, focusing on the new drink as if it held the secrets of the universe. This was dangerous territory, this easy slide back into the connection that had once felt as natural as breathing. He'd bought me a drink. I'd smiled. Such seemingly simple gestures, but they were anything but.

When I looked up again, he was walking toward the door, his apron left behind. Disappointment settled in my chest like a stone, which made no sense at all. I'd told him I couldn't do this, that seeing him was too painful. He was respecting my wishes, giving me the space I'd demanded.

So why did I feel bereft as I watched him leave without saying goodbye?

Through the window, I watched him climb into a truck parked across the street. The engine started, the headlights cut through the evening dusk, and then he was gone. Only then did I realize I'd been holding my breath.

I finished my wine with more haste than wisdom and gathered my purse. The restaurant had emptied considerably, but the bar was still full.

I waved at Keltie as I made my way to the same door JW had left through.

Her smile was warm when she came around to say hello. "Echo! I didn't even see you come in. How was your evening?"

I gave her a quick hug. "I knew you were busy. How are you? How's Luna?"

"The happiest little girl in the world." She hugged me once more. Tighter. We'd been through a lot together as her daughter fought against leukemia. Her continued remission was something I still prayed for every day.

"Tell her Miss Echo said hello." I waved behind me and stepped out into the cool mountain air. My house was only two blocks away, past other Victorian cottages with their welcoming porch lights and the community gardens where neighbors grew vegetables and flowers side by side. Normal sights in a normal town where I'd built a normal life.

But nothing felt normal anymore.

My house sat on a quiet street, a small craftsman bungalow with a garden I'd spent years perfecting. Inside, the familiar surroundings that usually brought me peace—books stacked on the coffee table, a mug in the sink from my morning coffee, the cozy accumulation of a life lived alone but not lonely—felt hollow tonight. The silence oppressive.

I poured a glass of water and sat at my kitchen table, forcing myself to think clearly through the alcohol and the emotional chaos of the day. Even if I wanted to spend time with JW—which I absolutely did not—it was impossible. Too much had happened after he left, too many decisions made and consequences lived with. If I told him what my life had been like then, the choices I'd been forced to make, whatever fragile connection we might rebuild would crumble into nothing.

It wasn't about protecting myself. It never had been. It had always been about protecting everyone else.

When I finally crawled into bed, sleep eluded me. My mind replayed the day's events in an endless loop. Every time I closed my eyes, I saw JW's face in the crowd during the parade, the shock of recognition that had shaken us both. The way he'd spoken my name, gentle and hesitant. The hurt in his eyes when I'd fled from him at the river.

Dreams came in fragments when I finally dozed—dancing as strong arms held me close, whispered promises of forever that turned into dust.

By six, I'd given up on rest. I showered and dressed, needing the comfort of familiar habits. Whatever emotional chaos JW's return had triggered, I couldn't let it affect my work. The children and families who depended on Miracles of Hope deserved better than a director distracted by her past.

I walked to the coffee shop as I did every day, the mountain air crisp with birdsong mixing with the distant hum of early traffic. The bell chimed as I entered, and my steps faltered.

JW sat at a table near the window, reading what looked like the local newspaper, a steaming mug beside his elbow. The sound of the bell made him look up, and our eyes met briefly. He'd dressed casually in jeans and a button-down shirt that brought out the green in his eyes. I saw him hesitate, as if debating whether to acknowledge me.

I looked away quickly, my hands unsteady as I approached the counter. The barista called out my usual order before I'd even asked, saving me from having to speak. My fingers fumbled with my wallet as I paid, hyperaware of JW's presence across the room.

"Thank you," I managed.

"Have a good day, Maya." I heard as I approached the door. It was a simple courtesy, but spoken in JW's voice, it felt like more.

"You too," I said, hurrying out in the direction of my office, coffee sloshing in my cup.

Would every encounter feel this charged? This was a small town—now that we'd come face-to-face, recognized each other, we were bound to meet up again. I needed to develop better coping mechanisms than unsteady hands and shallow breathing.

The weekend brought no respite. Saturday's farmer's market proved my concerns were justified. I was selecting peaches from a stand when I spotted JW examining tomatoes two stalls down.

I paid for my fruit and rushed toward my car, but not before catching his eye across the market. He lifted his hand in a small wave, and despite myself, I returned the gesture. Just politeness between old acquaintances who happened to live in the same small town. But tension coiled in my stomach as I drove home.

The encounters continued through the week, each one seeming coincidental but leaving me rattled—JW at the grocery store, outside the post office, walking down the opposite side of Elk Avenue.

Wednesday brought the most challenging test yet. I was meeting Misty and Dr. Cressman at the Goat to discuss the hospital's partnership with our foundation when I spotted JW having lunch alone at the table near the back where I'd been sitting the night of the fourth.

He didn't approach our table, didn't interrupt our conversation. Just ate his meal quietly, nodded politely when our eyes met, and left before we did. But I was distracted the entire time, catching myself stealing looks in his direction.

"You seem jumpy," Misty observed as we walked to our cars. "Is work overwhelming you?"

"Just the usual summer chaos," I deflected, forcing a smile. "Too many cases, not enough hours in the day."

She didn't look convinced but let it go. What could I tell her? That seeing my former lover—if that inadequate term even applied to what we'd been—was slowly dismantling the equilibrium I'd built my life around?

The week wore on with increasing strain. I began changing my routines, taking different routes to avoid potential encounters. The coffee shop became off-limits. I shopped for groceries at odd hours, but I couldn't avoid the bank, and on Friday morning, we met up again. He'd walked in right before me and was already in line. He turned when the door chimed, and his face brightened.

"Maya…er…Echo." He stepped aside, gesturing for me to go ahead of him in line. "Please."

"That's not necessary," I protested, but he was already moving to let me pass.

"I insist. I'm not in any hurry."

The casual kindness undid me more than dramatic gestures might have. This was the JW I remembered—considerate without fanfare, thoughtful in small ways that mattered.

"Have a good weekend," he said as I passed him on my way out.

That afternoon, I drove to the Slate River, seeking the solitude and clarity that mountain water had always provided. Most people were still at work, so the trail was empty. I settled on the boulder where I'd sat after the parade, letting the sound of rushing water calm my racing thoughts.

I was so lost in meditation that I didn't notice him approaching until I heard him speak. "I hoped I might find you here."

When I opened my eyes, JW was standing at the edge of the clearing, with his hands in his pockets.

"This used to be our place," I said, the words escaping before I could stop them.

"It could still be." He moved closer, but remained a couple of feet away, respecting the invisible boundary I'd drawn around myself. "If you'd let it."

"JW—" I started, then stopped. What could I say? That seeing him kept rattling me? That I thought about him more than I should, remembered things I'd sworn to forget?

"I heard what you said the other day." His voice was gentle. "But I can't stop hoping your feelings might change."

"Why?" The question burst out of me, raw with weeks of confusion. "You left. Why are you here now? What do you want from me?"

"Because I never stopped thinking about you." The admission hung between us, stark and honest. "Not for a single day in all these years."

"You know nothing about me," I whispered. "We're different people now."

He took a step closer. "Let me get to know you again."

The request terrified me more than anger or demands might have. He wasn't pushing, wasn't trying to force his way back into my life. He was just asking to know me.

"I can't." The words came out broken, heavy with what I couldn't explain.

"Why not?"

Because there were things I could never share. Because letting him back in would mean risking what I'd built on the foundation of his absence.

When I shook my head, he studied me.

"Please, Maya. It doesn't have to be complicated. We would meet for coffee sometime. Maybe have a conversation that lasts longer than thirty seconds."

"I need time," I said.

"I'll wait. As long as you need."

He started to walk away, then paused. "I'm sorry for leaving the way I did, for not explaining. I'm sorrier than you'll ever know."

Then he was gone, leaving me alone with the sound of rushing water and the terrible knowledge that my defenses were deteriorating. Every encounter, every polite exchange, every moment of casual kindness was wearing away at the barriers I'd built around my heart.

What scared me wasn't that he might give up and leave again. More, it was that I was weakening, that I might not be strong enough to withstand the pull of what we'd once been.

If I gave in, I'd have to tell him all the things I knew I never could.

15

When I walked in several days later, the Goat felt different than it had on the Fourth of July—quieter, with the lunch rush long past and only a few scattered patrons nursing drinks at the bar. Victor was behind the register, counting receipts. When he looked up and saw me enter, his weathered face creased into a smile.

"JW. What brings you by this afternoon?"

I glanced around the nearly empty restaurant, noting that Keltie was nowhere to be seen. "I was hoping we could talk. About Maya—I mean Echo."

Victor set down his pen and studied my face. He gestured toward a corner booth, the same one where Echo had sat that night after the parade. "Want some coffee?"

"Please."

Before he returned with two steaming mugs, I noticed Keltie had come out from the kitchen to take his place.

"Is this a bad time?" I asked when he settled across from me.

"Not at all. I was getting ready to take a break anyway. So, you and Echo?"

I nodded.

"The two of you have been dancing around each other since the parade. What's going on?"

"I don't know how to approach her," I admitted. "Every time we talk, she shuts down. Every casual encounter in town leaves her looking like she wants to run."

Victor studied my face with the same intensity he had when I was a young buck he was attempting to teach about life. "You know, I remember you together. You reminded me of me and my wife when we first met."

My hands stilled around the coffee mug. "Victor—"

"No, let me say this." He leaned forward, lowering his tone. "I saw what you had. The way she'd look for you when she came to work, how her whole face would light up when you walked into a room. And you—hell, son, you looked at that girl like she hung the moon."

I couldn't meet his eyes. The memories his words evoked cut too deep. "I know what we had. That's what makes this so hard."

"What you don't know is what happened after you left."

My blood chilled, thinking back on her saying I'd destroyed her. "What do you mean?"

Victor's expression darkened. "Echo didn't just lose her boyfriend, JW. That girl was completely broken."

I forced myself to ask the question I dreaded. "How bad was it?"

He shook his head slowly. "Terrible. At first, she continued coming to work, but was only going through the motions. She'd stare out the window during her shifts. Customers would have to call her name three times before she'd notice them."

The coffee turned bitter in my mouth. I set the mug down with unsteady hands. "How long did this go on?"

"For a while. Then one day, she called and said she was sorry, but she couldn't work here anymore."

"No notice?"

"Even if she'd given it, I would've paid her severance and told her she didn't need to return. I knew how hard being here was for her."

"What else, Victor?"

"She disappeared for months. When she finally came back to Crested Butte, she was different." He leaned back in the booth. "Stronger, somehow. Like she'd found her backbone while she was away. But there was a sadness in her that wasn't there before. A guardedness."

"Did she return to work?"

"No. Right after, I sold the Goat to the Rice family and moved to Albuquerque."

"God, I—"

He held up a hand. "I'm not telling you this to make you feel guilty, JW. Well, maybe a little." His manner grew firmer. "You said she shuts down when you see her. This is why."

"She won't even give me a chance to explain."

"Can you blame her?" His question was gentle but pointed. "From her perspective, you left without a trace. No goodbye, no explanation, no contact. I know you had no choice, but that had no bearing on how she was affected."

I rubbed my temples, feeling the familiar burden of decades-old regret. "I want her to know why—"

"Then, tell her."

"How can I when she won't listen?"

Victor leaned forward again. "JW, I've known you since you were born. I watched you build a life from nothing, seen you carry burdens that would break most men. You are strong enough to get through to her."

"But—"

He cocked his head and raised a brow. "You know, when I first saw her at Children's Hospital—when Luna was so sick—I didn't recognize her. Didn't put two and two together."

"You had a lot on your mind."

"That, and I knew her as Maya Zaneta, not Echo West."

"West?" I thought back to when Flynn introduced us, but couldn't recall if she'd said a last name. She was married? No. She couldn't be. I would've noticed a ring, and even if she didn't wear one, I was sure she would've told me.

"From what I've heard, she was married a long time ago, but it didn't last long."

The thought of Echo married to someone else sent a spike of jealousy through me that I had no right to feel. "Victor, what should I do?"

"Be honest with her. Tell her everything. And then be patient." He reached across the table and gripped my shoulder. "Don't give up on her, JW. What you had is worth fighting for. *She's* worth fighting for." He looked up at the clock. "Break time's over."

We embraced, and I thanked him, then spent the rest of the afternoon walking the streets of Crested Butte, his words echoing in my mind.

By evening, I'd made my decision. I had to tell her what had happened all those years ago, even if I had to beg her to listen.

I found her at the farmer's market a few days later, purchasing vegetables at a produce stand.

"Echo," I said, reminding myself that was who she was now. Not Maya. "I was hoping we could talk."

"JW—"

"Please. There are things you need to know. Things that might help you understand why I left."

She studied me for a long moment, then glanced around at the bustling market. "Not here."

"Wherever you're comfortable."

"There's a park near the school. It's usually quiet this time of day."

Since it was only a few blocks away, we walked but didn't speak.

"What did you want to tell me?" she asked fifteen minutes later when we sat at a picnic table.

I took a deep breath, knowing that what I said next would either begin to heal the rift between us or destroy any chance we might have had.

"My name is John William Rooker," I began. "You knew me as John Williams. When I had to disappear, I changed it to Javier Wyatt."

Her eyebrows rose. "Why? I mean, why so many different names?"

"For protection." I looked out over the valley, gathering the courage for what came next. "The woman you know as Patricia Wheaton—Flynn's mother—was my aunt. My father's sister."

I explained about Patricia and why I really had to leave all those years ago. About my father's attempt to force her to end her pregnancy, about Cena Covert and her arranging for a place for Patricia to live in Colorado. I told her about the years I'd spent protecting her family from the shadows, watching over children who hadn't known who I was until recently or the secret role I'd played in their lives.

When the story ended, Echo didn't say anything for several minutes.

"So you didn't even tell me your real name," she finally said.

"JW was close. It's what everyone called me, then and now." I shook my head. "Sorry. You're right. I didn't. I lied to you."

She turned to face me fully. "Why? When we were together, when we were making plans—why couldn't you trust me?"

My voice caught, and I had to clear my throat before I could answer. "Because I was eighteen when we came here, and I'd been taught that our safety—Patricia's safety—depended on never telling anyone who we really were. By the time I understood that you could be trusted, that you were someone I wanted to share everything with, it was too late."

"Too late, how?"

"My brother was getting close to finding us, and that meant staying would put you in danger. And if I'd told you what was happening, you might have insisted on coming with us, and I couldn't ask you to give up your whole life for someone who was essentially living a lie."

She stood and walked a few feet away, her back to me. "You made that choice for both of us."

"Yes. And it was wrong." The admission reopened old wounds. "I should have told you everything. Given you the option to decide for yourself."

"Do you have any idea what it was like?" She turned to face me. "One day, we're talking about our future, and the next, you were just gone."

I stood abruptly, took a step toward her, then stopped myself. My hands hung uselessly at my sides. "I loved you more than I've ever loved anyone. Leaving you was the hardest thing I've ever done."

"But you still did it."

"I told myself I was protecting you. From my father, from the complications of my life, from having to live in hiding." I moved closer, though I didn't try to touch her. "I was wrong."

She wiped at her eyes with the back of her hand. "Why are you telling me this now? Why are you even here?"

"Because the obligations that kept me away are finished. Because I never stopped thinking about you. And when I saw you at the parade, I felt like fate was giving us another chance."

"I need time to think. Even after I have, I can't say for sure that I'll want to see you."

"I understand."

My heart sank as I watched her walk away.

16

Echo

A week had passed since JW's revelation at the park. The lies he'd told—about his name, his past, his reasons for being in Crested Butte—felt like betrayals even as his explanations made sense. John William Rooker, not the JW I'd known. Patricia Wheaton's nephew, bound by promises and secrets that predated our relationship by years. His abandonment hadn't been about me at all. I was collateral damage.

I'd thrown myself into work, reviewing grant applications and visiting families whose children needed our support. The routine provided a distraction from my churning thoughts about JW and what his presence in my life might mean.

I was in the office earlier than usual when Melanie knocked on my door and stepped inside, waving an envelope addressed to Miracles of Hope. "This came in yesterday's mail. Anonymous donation. Pretty substantial."

I pulled out the contents after she'd handed it to me, and my eyes flared. Tucked into a folded sheet of paper was a cashier's check for fifty thousand dollars, made out to the charity. "In memory of Scarlett Blanche Wheaton," was in the memo line.

I read the accompanying note out loud. "This donation honors a little girl who fought bravely and the mother who never stopped loving her. May it help other families find hope in their darkest hours."

Scarlett Blanche. Patricia's first daughter, the child who'd died of leukemia before Flynn was born. Only someone with intimate knowledge of the family would know that name and understand its significance to the charity Patricia had founded in her memory.

I suspected it was from JW, but found it curious that he would give it anonymously rather than get the recognition and gratitude if it had been done publicly. That he'd chosen to honor Scarlett's memory quietly said a lot about his character.

"Thanks for showing this to me," I said, putting everything back in the envelope and holding it out to Melanie.

Over the following couple of weeks, I noticed JW around town several times. One morning, he was having breakfast at McGill's with Keltie and Holt, listening as Luna chattered about her upcoming school play. When baby Scarlett fussed, he gently bounced her while Luna showed him a drawing she'd made.

Another day, I saw him outside the grocery store with Flynn and her family. Paxon and Rooker were climbing on the wooden bear sculpture while Irish loaded bags into their SUV. JW held baby Rowan, bouncing her when she fussed.

Each sighting revealed the same thing. He'd slipped into the lives of people I cared about. The Wheaton family had embraced him as one of their own, and he fit in like he'd always been there.

When our paths crossed directly, his demeanor was always warm but respectful. A polite nod when we passed on the street. A courteous "good morning" at the post office. He never lingered, never pushed for conversation, never made me feel uncomfortable.

"Hey, Echo?" said Melanie, jarring my attention back to the case files I was reviewing.

I raised my hand, motioning for her to enter.

"Have you heard about the guy who's staying at the Roaring Fork?"

I shook my head.

"Rumor is he's related to the Wheatons. Anyway, I met him at the farmer's market last weekend, and honestly, I could barely form complete sentences." She laughed. "He's got long, silver-streaked hair, eyes I couldn't stop staring into, and that body. Not to mention he's sweet enough to help me carry my bags to my car when he noticed me struggling with them."

My grip on my pen was so tight my knuckles turned white.

"Someone else said he owns a ranch in New Mexico. I wonder if he's single." Melanie got up and left, apparently so taken with JW's memory that she didn't realize I hadn't said a word.

After she left, I sat staring out my office window. Despite my anger, despite my hurt, despite my decision to keep my distance, I wasn't as immune to his presence as I'd wanted to believe. The idea of JW with someone else, of him turning his attention toward another woman, set my teeth on edge. But I had no claim on him, no right to feel possessive about a man I'd been avoiding since I ran into him at the Fourth of July parade. Yet here I was, wanting to tell Melanie to stay the hell away from him.

Not that it had anything to do with her seeing JW at the farmer's market, I made it a point to visit the following Saturday. I was about to give up hope of seeing him and take my peaches home when the sound of laughter caught my attention. When I turned to look, I spotted JW with Flynn and her family. Paxon and Rooker raced ahead of the group, exploring the various stalls. Irish followed with the stroller, while Flynn and JW walked together.

I watched as they stopped at the produce stand next to mine. Paxon immediately gravitated toward JW, tugging on his jacket to show him a rock he'd found. Instead of brushing off the child's excitement, he knelt to Paxon's level.

"That's a perfect rock. You'll have to show me where you found it."

"Over there by the flowers!" Paxon pointed. "Rooker found one too, but mine's better."

"They're both excellent rocks."

When Rowan began fussing in her stroller while Flynn was paying for her purchases, JW lifted her out.

She calmed against his shoulder, her tiny hand fisting in his shirt as she dozed. Still, he listened to Paxon's and Rooker's chatter while soothing the baby, giving each child his attention.

"Echo!" I heard Flynn call out at the same time JW looked up. Our eyes met across the market, and neither of us blinked. When he approached, still carrying Rowan, I didn't budge.

"Hello," he said.

"Hello." I couldn't take my eyes off the baby in his arms, the way she seemed content against his chest. "Rowan likes you."

"The feeling's mutual." He adjusted her position. "How have you been?"

"Fine. Busy with work." I gestured toward my bag of peaches. "The usual."

We stood in awkward silence until he cleared his throat. "The Roaring Fork hosts a chuckwagon dinner for their guests every week. There's food, a campfire, music...I was wondering if you'd like to come out some time."

The invitation caught me off guard. "Oh, I, um, when's the next one?" The question escaped before I could stop it.

"Tonight, actually. Six o'clock." His eyebrows rose. "You're welcome to join us if you'd like."

I should have declined. Should have thanked him politely and made some excuse. "I'd love to," I blurted instead, before I could stop myself.

His face transformed. "Really?"

"Really." A smile tugged at my lips.

"Would you like me to pick you up? Say at five-thirty?"

"It's okay. I can drive out myself."

"Sure. Of course. You know the way, right?"

I smiled again. "I've been to the Roaring Fork many times."

"Good. Well, I guess I'll see you tonight."

"You will."

He turned to leave, but stopped and looked over his shoulder. "I'm really looking forward to it, Echo."

"Me too," I whispered once he was far enough away that he wouldn't hear me.

Just as I walked in the front door of my house, juggling groceries, my cell rang. I dropped my bags on the counter and dug it out of my purse, delighted when I saw my son's name flash on the screen.

"Hi, sweetheart. How are you? Are you in town?"

"Hey, Mom. Just got back and have a short break before I have to head out again. There's a reason they call this time of year Cowboy Christmas. Back-to-back-to-back events practically every weekend."

"How's it going?"

"Solid season so far. Our bulls are rank. That's about all we can ask for." That was Kingston—understated even about his successes.

"It's wonderful to have you home, sweetheart. I hope we can get together before you're out on the road again."

"That's actually why I called. There's a dinner at the Roaring Fork tonight, and Flynn's saying my presence is mandatory. I wish I could get into town to see you, but it isn't looking good. Any chance you could come out this way instead?"

"I'd love to," I said rather than admitting his was my second invitation.

I spent the rest of the afternoon nervous and second-guessing myself. I changed clothes three times, finally settling on dark jeans and a blue sweater. Not because I wanted to impress anyone, I told myself, despite the ten times I checked my makeup before leaving the house.

The drive to Roaring Fork Ranch felt both too long and too short. Part of me wanted to turn around and make excuses for missing dinner. But I'd committed to being there, and Kingston would wonder why I'd changed my mind.

The chuckwagon was set up in the meadow behind the main house, with picnic tables arranged around the cooking area and a large circle campfire already blazing. Ranch guests—families with children, couples, friends—mingled with the Wheaton family members under the lights that were strung between the trees.

Flynn hurried over when I climbed out of my car.

"Echo! I'm so glad you came." She pulled me into a hug. "You look beautiful."

"Thank you for having me."

"You're always welcome. You know that. Come on. Let me get you a drink."

As Flynn led me toward the group, I spotted Kingston near the fire pit. He was talking with Holt, but excused himself as soon as he saw me.

"I missed you, Mom," he said, wrapping me in a big hug.

"I missed you too, sweetheart."

He let go and glanced around at the crowd. "Nice turnout."

Flynn joined us with JW close behind. "Oh wonderful, Kingston, who everyone calls Bridger, is here! JW, you should meet Echo's son. Bridger, this is JW—the family friend I was telling you about."

"Pleasure," JW said, extending his hand.

My son nodded. "Heard fine things."

The dinner that followed was exactly what I'd hoped—a relaxing time with excellent food and company. During the meal, I found myself able to enjoy the conversation and atmosphere without the awkwardness I'd anticipated.

"Solid system you've got here," JW said to Kingston, who'd sat on the other side of him.

"Seems like it. My job revolves around the roughstock more and more. Didn't know they were even doin' this," he responded, motioning to the guests lined up to fill their plates a second time.

As the meal wound down, Holt brought out his guitar and found a spot near the campfire where logs had been arranged for seating. "Time for some music. Anyone else want to join in?"

My son left briefly and returned with his guitar case. I watched him settle beside Holt, tuning his instrument.

"Nice guitar," JW commented when we walked over to join them. "I have a Martin."

Kingston nodded.

"Hey, you play?" Holt asked.

"Yes, but sadly, I left my strings at the ranch."

Holt stood and walked over to his truck, pulling a case out of the back. "I always travel with an extra or two. Of course this isn't a Martin." He winked when he handed the Taylor to JW.

What followed was entertainment that made guest ranch experiences memorable. Holt led with country classics that guests could sing along to, while Kingston provided harmonies and instrumental support. His voice, when he did sing, commanded attention.

When JW joined in, the music transformed. His voice blended with theirs, creating rich harmony that elevated the songs. The three men found their rhythm quickly—putting on a great show for everyone there.

Ranch guests requested songs, and the guys obliged with everything from classic country to folk standards.

When they performed "Wagon Wheel," the entire crowd sang along. During a quieter moment, when they played an instrumental version of "Amazing Grace," I blinked back tears.

As things wound down and guests began drifting back toward their cabins, I realized I didn't want the night to end.

"I've got a four-AM wake-up call tomorrow," said Kingston. "Night, Mom. Glad you came." He walked over, hugged me, and kissed my cheek.

"Me too, sweetheart. The music was wonderful."

"Let's get together again before I have to leave."

"I'd like that," I said before looking around for Flynn and Cord to thank them for their hospitality.

After I had and was heading to my car, I heard footsteps on the gravel behind me. JW approached, hands in his pockets.

"Can I walk with you?"

I hesitated, then nodded. "That would be nice. Thanks."

The moon was bright overhead, casting everything in silver light. "It's a beautiful night."

"Is it?"

I turned to face him.

"I can't see anything beyond the gorgeous woman who kept me captivated for the last few hours."

I smiled. "You were always such a charmer."

JW put his hand on my arm, and we both stopped walking when we reached where I'd parked. "Only with you, Echo. I mean that."

"Thank you for this. It was wonderful," I said, pulling out my key fob.

He took a step closer. "Thank you for coming."

"You, Kingston, and Holt singing and playing together—that was special."

"Your son is a fine young man."

"Thank you…uh…I should be going."

"Echo, I—" he began, then stopped.

"What is it?"

Instead of answering, he took another tentative step closer. When I didn't retreat, he reached up, giving me every opportunity to pull away, and cupped my cheek.

"Is this all right?" he whispered.

I should have said no. Should have shaken my head, maintained the boundaries I'd spent weeks establishing. Instead, I leaned into his touch, my eyes closing at the warmth of his hand against my skin.

When I opened them, he lowered his head until his lips barely brushed mine.

The kiss was soft at first, tentative, a question asked without words. But when I didn't pull away, when my lips parted under his, it deepened. My hands fisted in his shirt, pulling him closer as weeks of denial and resistance crumbled.

This was what I'd been running from. Not just the memory of what we'd shared, but the knowledge that nothing had changed. I still responded to his touch, still felt complete when he held me.

He broke the kiss first, resting his forehead against mine as we both struggled to catch our breath.

"God, Echo, I'm—" he started.

But I couldn't bear to hear whatever he was going to say. Couldn't risk him apologizing for the kiss, or trying to explain what it meant, or worse—suggesting it had been a mistake.

I pressed two fingers to his lips, stopping him from speaking. "Good night, JW."

Then I slipped into my car and started the engine, leaving him standing in the moonlight as I drove away.

The miles home passed in a haze. My lips still tingled from his kiss. My body still hummed with the awareness of his touch. Every rational thought I'd constructed about why I couldn't risk letting him become a part of my life seemed inconsequential.

As I pulled into my driveway, one thought echoed in my mind—*what was I doing?*

But even as I asked the question, I knew the answer. I was falling for JW all over again, despite every reason why I should resist. Despite the secrets I carried, despite the complications his presence created, despite the very real possibility that letting him back into my heart would destroy the life I'd built.

I couldn't resist him. Never had been able to.

And even with all the warning bells ringing in my head, I wasn't sure I wanted to anymore.

17

The morning after our kiss, I woke before dawn with Echo's taste still on my lips and the memory of how she'd responded to me filling me with burning desire. She'd pulled me close with a passion that spoke of feelings she couldn't deny, then left after stopping me from saying things I knew I shouldn't.

Yesterday, Buck had called for all hands to help with the hay baling, so I grabbed my work gloves and headed to the barn. The mid-August heat was already building, promising another scorching day, but the mindless rhythm of physical labor would keep my thoughts from spinning in circles.

Buck, Cord, and Bridger were already in the field when I arrived, working alongside the ranch hands to get the equipment ready. We fell into the rhythm without much conversation—there was work to be done, and we all knew how to do it.

The morning passed in the steady routine of cutting, raking, and rolling. It wasn't until we were loading bales onto the truck that any of us had much time for a conversation.

"Hey, when do you head out again?" Cord asked Bridger.

"Four days."

Cord laughed and shook his head. "Like gettin' blood out of a stone. Where are you headin' next?"

"Rodeo de Taos, then up to Montana for the Big Timber Weekly, followed by the stampede."

"Taos is a well-respected event. It's been going on for over fifty years, if I remember correctly," I said, hefting another bale.

"This is the fifty-fifth," Bridger confirmed.

"What are you taking?" I asked.

"Bulls and broncs. We let the Rice boys handle the stock for the timed events," he responded.

"We decided early on that we didn't want to get into things like tie-downs, team-roping, or steer-wrestling," Cord said. "Although ol' Bridger here used to rank pretty good as a bulldogger."

"Too old for that shit now," he muttered.

Over the next two days of haying, our conversations expanded beyond the immediate work. Bridger talked about the circuit—the challenges of keeping livestock healthy on the road, the satisfaction of watching a good bull or bronc perform, and the business side of contracts and logistics.

"We're in the heart of the season now," he said as we secured the last load of the day. "I'll be on the road until October, home for a few days, then going right back out again."

Stunned at how forthcoming he was about his schedule—I'd rarely heard the man say more than two or three words at a time—I took it as an opening to an idea I'd been considering. "I have a ranch outside Taos. Sangre Vista. If you need a place for your operation to stay at during the event, you're welcome to use it."

Bridger's brow rose. "That's generous, but we couldn't impose—"

"It's not an imposition. I've got guest cabins, good pastures—everything you'd need."

He considered this, watching my reaction. "What would that run?"

"Nothing. One stockman helping another."

"I don't take charity."

"It's not charity. The place is just sitting there otherwise, and good livestock deserves proper care."

He nodded slowly. "If you're sure it wouldn't be putting you out."

"I'm sure."

That evening, I joined Flynn and the others in the ranch's office to give them feedback on how I thought their guest ranch operation was going, along with suggestions for the next step to grow if they were ready. The discussion eventually turned to my travel schedule.

"I'll need to head back to New Mexico for a week or two," I said. "Some business to handle at Sangre Vista, and I've offered to let Bridger and his crew stay there during the Taos rodeo."

"You're leaving?" Flynn asked.

The vulnerability in her words reminded me how much our family connection meant to her. "Just temporarily. I promise I'll be back."

"I know, but…" She hesitated.

"Hey, you've got all of us, sis," said Cord, rubbing her shoulder. "Not to mention Irish."

She shot him a look. "I haven't forgotten any of you, especially my husband. It's just that…" Tears pooled in her eyes, and she looked away.

I stood, offered my hand, and led her from the office. Once we were out of earshot, I motioned to a hay bale, and we both took a seat. "What's this about, Flynn?"

"Nothing. I'm just being silly."

"Look at me." I waited several seconds until she did, then spoke again. "You have become like a daughter to me, and your kids, like grandchildren. You have no idea how important you and the rest of your family are to me. I have no intention of giving that up. And when you're sick of me being around all the time, it'll be too late. You're never getting rid of me."

She smiled and wiped at her tears. "Grandchildren, huh? Maybe they should start calling you that, instead of uncle."

I put my hand on my heart. "I would love that," I said, my voice clogged with emotion.

"Pretty soon, there will be four calling you that, instead of three." Flynn rested her hand on her stomach. "Or five if I have twins again."

"Really? That's wonderful." I pulled her into my arms and hugged her. "You are such a good mother, Flynn."

"Am I?"

Her vulnerability and emotional responses meant more to me now that I knew she was pregnant. "Yes, you are warm, loving, nurturing, and gentle. It all shows in your children's happiness. Your mother would be so proud of you."

Her eyes filled with tears again that she quickly brushed away. "So what about you?"

"I fear my child-rearing years are over," I said, patting my stomach like she had.

Flynn nudged me. "You're hysterical. But be serious for a minute. What about you and Echo?"

I sighed. "It is very complicated."

"That kiss wasn't."

"Spying again?"

"Maybe, but quit trying to change the subject. You should invite her to Sangre Vista."

I hadn't seen the suggestion coming and wasn't sure what to say.

"Think about it. She hardly gets to see Bridger when he's on the road. She can see your ranch and spend time with her son."

Cord approached from the other room. "She's got a point. Sometimes, a change of scenery helps people see things differently."

Again, I was stunned. Were all of the Wheaton siblings aware of my feelings for Echo?

"I don't know," I said. "She's—"

"The worst she can say is no," Flynn pressed.

An hour later, sitting on my cabin's porch, I seriously considered Flynn's suggestion. Sangre Vista had always been my sanctuary, the place where I could be myself even in the face of my obligations to Patricia's family. If Echo and I were going to find our way forward, maybe that's what we needed.

I pulled out my phone and dialed before I could second-guess myself.

"Hello?"

"Echo, it's JW. I hope I'm not calling too late."

"No, it's fine. What's up?"

"I'm helping out at the Goat tonight—they're short-staffed for the weekend rush. I was wondering if you might want to stop by."

Silence stretched between us. "I don't know..."

"No pressure."

A longer silence. "I might. No promises."

"Of course. Hope to see you."

I was behind the bar when Echo walked through the door. She was wearing dark jeans and a pearl-snap shirt that brought out her coloring as much as her outfit hugged her curves. My hands fumbled with the glass I was drying when I thought about how it used to feel to have her naked body next to mine.

For the next hour, I stole glances in her direction while I mixed drinks and poured beer. Victor was at the end of the bar closest to where she sat, but I could eavesdrop and watch how her face lit up when he told her about Luna's upcoming school play—watching her in this space where we'd first fallen in love stirred memories I thought I'd buried.

During a brief lull, I rounded the bar and walked down to the end where she sat talking to Keltie, who'd given her dad a break. "Can I steal you away for a minute?"

Echo looked hesitant at first but followed me out to the restaurant's small patio.

"Nice evening," I said, gesturing toward the butte silhouetted against the night sky.

"It is." She wrapped her arms around herself against the chill. "Was there something you wanted to talk to me about?"

I took a breath, deciding to be direct. "Bridger's coming to stay at my ranch next week during the Taos rodeo. I was wondering if you'd like to come visit for a few days."

Her eyes flared. "Visit your ranch?"

"Yes." I thought about suggesting it would be good to get away from the memories here and maybe get a fresh start, but decided it would be better not to push.

"That's very kind, but I don't think it's a good idea."

The rejection stung, but I steeled my reaction. "I understand. Maybe some other time."

"Maybe."

We returned inside, and Echo rejoined Keltie and Victor while I went back to my duties. As the evening wound down and the last customers filtered out, I noticed Echo lingering at the bar, in no hurry to leave.

"Another drink?" I asked as I wiped down glasses.

"No, thank you." She traced patterns on the bar's wooden surface. "JW?"

"Yeah?"

"About your invitation…" Her eyes bored into mine. "I've changed my mind."

I nearly dropped the glass I was holding. "Really?"

"Yes. If the offer's still open."

"Of course it is. I was planning on leaving tomorrow afternoon, but—"

"I'll be ready. I mean, if it's okay if I travel with you."

I wanted to jump with joy, kick my heels together, and punch my fist in the air. Instead, I said, "That would be very nice."

The drive to Sangre Vista took most of the next day, winding through mountain passes and high desert valleys that gradually transformed from Colorado's familiar peaks to New Mexico's broader vistas. Echo and I discussed her current duties, my plans for expanding the ranch operations, books we'd been reading, places we wanted to travel—exchanges that felt natural despite the years between us.

"Tell me about Sangre Vista," she said as we crossed the state line and the landscape opened into wider valleys dotted with sagebrush and juniper.

"Cena Covert found the land. Remote enough for privacy and beautiful enough to share with others eventually. When I first saw it, I knew it could become home."

"Was it difficult? Building from scratch?"

"The best kind of challenge. Every fence post, every trail, every building—I could see the ranch's future taking shape." I glanced at her as we began the climb into the Sangre de Cristo foothills. "Watch the trees change as we go higher. Pinyon and juniper give way to ponderosa, then Douglas fir and aspen near the peaks."

The elevation made itself known gradually—the air thinning, our breathing deepening, and the engine working harder as we climbed from 6,000 feet toward the ranch's 7,200-foot base elevation. Echo rolled down her window, breathing in the warm mountain air scented with pine resin and the sweet fragrance of late-summer wildflowers.

"It's different from the Rockies," she observed. "More spacious, yet equally as breathtaking."

"Wait until you see the sunrises and sunsets. Sangre de Cristos means 'Blood of Christ,' and at certain times of the day, the peaks turn crimson."

As we turned onto the ranch's private road, marked only by a discreet wooden sign and electronic gate, the landscape became more intimate. The road wound through groves of aspens, whose leaves shimmered silver-green in the afternoon breeze. A small stream paralleled our route, its water clear and quick over smooth stones, catching the late-August sunlight in dancing sparkles.

"JW," she breathed as we crested the final rise and my land spread before us. "This is incredible."

The main lodge sat nestled against a hillside like it had grown from the mountain itself, its river rock and timber construction blending seamlessly with the surrounding pines. Beyond the lodge, the cabins dotted a ridge overlooking the valley, each designed to capture the mountain views while maintaining privacy. Late-summer wildflowers—Indian paintbrush, lupine, and mountain asters—created splashes of color in the meadows that stretched toward the distant peaks.

I was stunned speechless by how much I'd missed it. Until this year, I'd never been gone for more than two or three weeks at a time. Now, the eight months felt more like years.

As we pulled up to the entrance, satisfaction spread through my chest. I wanted Echo to see what I'd accomplished, to understand the man I'd become. This wasn't inherited wealth or a family legacy—this was something I'd built with my own hands and vision.

"Welcome to Sangre Vista," I said, looking over at the woman whose beauty rivaled the views that took my breath away. "Ready?" I asked, cutting the engine.

Echo reached across the console and touched my hand. "Thank you for bringing me here."

Before she could pull away, I wrapped my fingers around hers and brought them to my lips. "I've dreamed of this day, but never imagined it would actually come true."

I got out, came around, and opened her door, offering my hand. At the same time, Sarah approached us.

"Welcome back, JW," she said. "Per your request, Pueblo Moon has been prepared for your guest."

I introduced my guest-services director to Echo, then confirmed Rick had the west barn and pasture ready for the stock when Bridger arrived, as well as the cabins ready for him and his crew.

"Everything has been taken care of," Sarah confirmed before turning to Echo. "I'd be happy to show you to your cabin if you'd like, Ms. West," Sarah offered, glancing between us. In fifteen years of operating the guest ranch, I'd never brought a woman here as a personal guest.

"I'll take care of it," I said, thanking Sarah before taking Echo's hand and leading her down the path bordered by native grasses and late-blooming columbines. "Flynn and her family stayed here over the holidays. This cabin was their home for a month."

Echo studied me with interest. "They must have loved it here."

"They did. The boys, especially." I chuckled, remembering their exuberance and excitement over every new thing they discovered.

"You're good with them."

I'd asked Flynn for permission to share her good news with Echo when I reported back to say her suggestion had worked. She'd hugged me so hard that I could still feel her arms around me. "They call me Grandpa JW now." My voice cracked, and I laughed, brushing away a tear. "I never thought anyone would…"

Echo squeezed my hand. "It suits you."

I raised a brow, unable to wipe the grin brought on by my happiness that she was here with me from my face.

"Grandpa JW. I like it," she added.

"I hope you'll be comfortable here," I said, leading her into the cabin that sat on the eastern ridge, positioned to capture both the sunrise views and the afternoon light across the valley. I opened the door to reveal the river-rock fireplace ready for evening use, the artisan-crafted furniture arranged to frame the mountain views, and the fresh flowers—Cora's touch—brightening the space with native Indian paintbrush and white delphiniums.

"The kitchen is fully stocked," I explained, "but Chef Alton has prepared a welcome dinner if you'd prefer to join me in the main lodge. The hot springs are perfect for evening soaks, and we have mountain bikes and hiking gear available if you're interested in exploring the trails."

Echo moved to the picture window, her reflection ghosted against the darkening mountain landscape. "This view..."

"Wait until morning," I said, wishing so much that I could be here, waking up with her in my arms, to show her how magical the mountains were at that time of day.

We spent the next three days exploring the ranch—sometimes on horseback through the network of trails I'd carved through forty miles of wilderness. I showed her the high meadows, where cattle grazed among scattered stands of aspens and pine; the private lake, where guests fished for native trout; the observatory dome, where we gathered for stargazing sessions under New Mexico's famously clear skies.

Each location held memories of building this place during my years of solitude after my mother's death—the satisfaction of problem-solving, the physical exhaustion that helped quiet grief, the gradual understanding that I was creating not just a business but a sanctuary. My time away brought it all back to me as if I was seeing it for the first time.

"You can see your pride in every detail," Echo said as we stood at Sunset Point, watching the peaks turn crimson in the fading light. "The trail maintenance, the way the buildings sit in the landscape, even how the staff moves through their routines. This isn't just a business—it's a work of art."

Her understanding meant more than I'd expected. "During my years of watching and waiting, ready to fulfill my promise to Patricia, the ranch gave me purpose."

The next day's ride took us out farther, and as we returned on the trail that led through pine forests dappled with afternoon sunlight, our horses' hooves were rhythmic on the well-maintained trails and the warm air carried the scent of wildflowers and summer grasses. Rick had chosen our mounts perfectly. Echo's especially.

"The Appaloosa suits you," I said to her as we approached the stables.

"She's lovely. Patient with my rustiness." Echo patted her animal's neck as we dismounted. "How many do you keep?"

"Twenty-six in the main stables, plus the string we use for guest rides. Rick manages the breeding program—we're developing a line particularly suited to high-altitude trail riding."

The man appeared, his smile brightening when he saw Echo. "How did you enjoy the sunset ride?"

"Magical," she replied. "I can see why guests fall in love with this place."

"We have a full-moon excursion planned for tomorrow night if you're interested. The valley looks magical under moonlight, and August is perfect weather for evening rides."

"We'll talk it over," I told him before thanking him and leading Echo toward the lodge. Selfishly, I didn't want to share her with a group of guests, but I would if it was what she wanted. I'd do anything she wanted, I realized. Anything. The thought was sobering but also grounding. I only prayed that Echo felt our connection to the same degree I was.

My staff could barely hide their curiosity about her presence. Cora lingered while arranging fresh flowers for Echo's cabin, her motherly attention more focused than usual. Michael found reasons to check the cabin's heating system twice. Even Alton mentioned special menu preparations with unusual enthusiasm.

"She seems lovely," Cora commented, gathering fresh towels and linens to deliver to Echo's cabin.

"She is."

"Known her long?"

"A lifetime." I watched Cora process this information with the discretion that had made her invaluable over the years. "We knew each other when we were young. Before all this."

Cora nodded, understanding more than she said. "It's good to see you happy, Javier."

Her use of the name I no longer needed was a jarring reminder that, eventually, I had to tell the staff the same story of my life I'd told Echo. Perhaps not in such detail, but they deserved an explanation.

Bridger and his crew arrived as the sun was setting, their trucks and trailers dusty from the road. The animals were restless even after what had to have been a short haul compared to what they were used to. I helped the guys get settled in the guest cabins I'd prepared and showed them the pastures where their stock could rest and recover before the competition.

"This is generous as hell," Bridger said as we finished securing the bulls for the night. "You sure there's nothing I can do to repay you? I know the Wheatons feel the same way."

"Having you here is payment enough," I said, squeezing his shoulder. "We have another special guest with us. I'm not sure if anyone made you aware."

He cocked his head. "Who?"

"Your mother."

His eyebrows flared, and he was momentarily speechless. "You're kidding," he finally said. "I can't believe she arranged to be here."

"It was at my suggestion."

His scrunched eyes met mine, and he put one hand on his hip. "Is there something you're trying to tell me?"

"Only that your mom and I knew each other many years ago. Reconnecting since I've been in Crested Butte has allowed us to renew our friendship."

His eyes tightened. "Friendship?"

"For now, yes."

He nodded once, then walked away. He'd only gotten a few steps before he turned around, pointing a finger in my direction. "Hurt her and I'll kill you."

I nodded like he had. "Understood. And what if I make her happy?"

"She deserves that," he murmured before continuing on the path to the cabins.

Over dinner that night, I observed Echo interacting with her son and his team. There was clear pride in her demeanor as she listened to them discuss how they'd done in Taos, their plans for the upcoming events, and the reputation they were building for providing quality animals. The easy affection between mother and son was obvious. Bridger was different around her. Willing to say more than a few words. I'd even seen him smile several times.

When we said good night, I suggested he walk her to Pueblo Moon while I stayed behind to "catch up on correspondence," even though there was really nothing I needed to do. My staff had managed this place the same as if I'd been here to oversee it. There was a time when that might not have filled me with the same relief I felt now. Perhaps, if things progressed as I hoped they would with Echo, I might be able to spend more time in Crested Butte than I'd thought.

I walked outside and rested my hands on the lodge's porch rail, looking up at the night sky and wondering if I could dare to hope, dare to dream.

18

Echo

The following night, as we walked toward Pueblo Moon under the star-filled sky, I remembered the donation that had arrived at the charity weeks ago. The timing, the specific mention of the little girl—it had been weighing on my mind since the day we got it.

"The Miracles of Hope received a generous but anonymous gift. Fifty thousand dollars in memory of Scarlett Blanche Wheaton," I said.

JW's steps slowed. "Oh?"

"It was you, wasn't it?"

He stopped walking and turned to face me directly. For a moment, I thought he might deny it. Instead, he asked, "What makes you think that?"

"Because you're the only person I've met recently who would know that name and understand what it would mean to the organization."

"Yes," he said simply. "It was me."

"Why anonymously?" I asked, genuinely curious. "Most donors want the recognition, especially for that amount."

"Because it wasn't about that. It was about honoring a little girl who never got the chance to grow up."

His words hit me unexpectedly hard. The quiet reverence in his voice, the way he spoke about a child whose memory he carried—made my throat tight with emotion.

"You really loved her, didn't you? Patricia."

"Like a sister. We went through everything together."

I studied his profile in the moonlight. "I'm beginning to understand the sacrifices you made for her family."

Here was a man who'd spent thirty years of his life protecting people who didn't even know who he was, who'd given up his own happiness to ensure theirs. Whatever anger I'd carried about his abandonment was slowly being replaced by something else—respect, understanding, maybe even the beginnings of forgiveness.

"Would you like to come in?" I asked when we stepped onto the porch.

"More than anything."

While I'd expected he would, since the night of the campfire, JW hadn't kissed me. Hadn't even come close. Rather than wait any longer, I reached for his hand, leaned up, and softly brushed his lips with mine.

"What was that for?" he asked.

"I got tired of waiting."

He raised a brow. "I wasn't sure you—"

Rather than let him finish, I kissed him again. The moment our mouths touched, something ignited between us. He wrapped his arm around my waist and pulled my body close to his. The taste of him was exactly as I remembered—not from that night, but from those kisses that had haunted my dreams for years. It was full of passion and heat and promise, and as much as I knew it was wrong, nothing had ever felt so right.

He broke the kiss first, looking into my eyes for answers to questions he hadn't asked.

"Come in," I said, unlocking the door, then waiting for him to open it. "I'm going to have a glass of wine. Would you like to join me?"

"I'd love to." His voice was soft, hesitant, and not at all what I wanted from him. And that wasn't fair.

While I poured our wine, JW lit the kindling in the fireplace. When I sat on the sofa, he sat beside me, and I turned to face him.

The past few days at Sangre Vista had shown me glimpses of the man he'd become—thoughtful, accomplished, deeply caring. Being here, seeing what he'd built, watching how his staff clearly respected and cared for him, was reshaping everything I thought I knew about the person who'd left me all those years ago.

"Echo," he said, setting his glass on the table in front of us. "There's something I need to tell you."

I tensed, now wishing I hadn't invited him in, wishing I hadn't kissed him. The firelight played across his features, highlighting the silver in his hair and the lines around his eyes that spoke of years I hadn't shared with him. "It's okay. You don't have to—"

"Let me say this. I want you in my life." His words were clear and unwavering. "I never stopped loving you—not for a single day in all these years. If there's any chance you could forgive me for leaving the way I did, I'll do anything to be with you."

His declaration, laying his heart bare, took my breath away. The vulnerability in his voice, the hope and fear warring in his expression—it was everything I'd once dreamed of hearing and everything I feared most.

I turned away and stared into the fire as my mind raced. Part of me wanted to throw caution aside, to tell him that I'd never stopped loving him either, that seeing him again had awakened feelings I'd thought were buried forever. But the practical part of me, the part that knew more lives than mine would be destroyed if I gave in, held me back.

There were still so many things he didn't know about what had happened after he left. Decisions I'd made, consequences I'd lived with, secrets I'd carried for nearly three decades. If I let him back into my heart completely, those truths would eventually surface. And when they did, would our love survive them?

"I'm sorry…I can't…I need more time," I finally said, standing. The words felt inadequate for the magnitude of what he'd just shared, but they were all I could manage.

"Of course." He stood too and walked to the door.

"Good night, JW," I said as I closed it behind him.

Once he was gone, I paced the small living area as my mind churned. These days at his ranch had shown me a life I could barely have imagined—beauty, peace, a sense of purpose and accomplishment that radiated from everything he'd created. He was offering me a place in that life, a chance to build something together that we'd only dreamed about when we were young. But dreams were easier than reality. In my case, reality came crashing in the moment I let it. Not only couldn't I allow JW to get any closer, but I couldn't stay here any longer. I was about to pick up my phone to call Kingston when it rang with what I recognized as the charity's emergency-line number, programmed to forward to my phone.

"Echo West," I answered.

"Echo, thank God you picked up." It was Melanie, and the strain in her voice made my stomach clench. "I'm so sorry to call. I know you're away, but we have a situation. Carley Wheeler—you remember the family—she's taken a turn for the worse."

Carley. Seven years old and had been fighting leukemia for two years. Her parents, Amy and Steve, had been pillars of strength through her treatment, but I could hear in Melanie's voice that something had changed.

"What happened?"

"She spiked a fever this afternoon, and her counts dropped dramatically. They've admitted her into the ICU. Her parents are…" Melanie's voice broke. "They're asking for you specifically."

I'd promised them that if they needed me, I would come as fast as I could. It was what we did at Miracles of Hope—we walked alongside families through the darkest moments of their lives. But Carley's case was particularly close to my heart. She reminded me of another little girl I'd once known, another fight that had been lost.

"I'm in New Mexico," I said, already moving toward my suitcase. "But I'll be back as quickly as I can. Where are they?"

"Denver. At Children's Hospital."

The logistics of getting there hit me as soon as I spoke. I'd have to find a way to the nearest airport, pray there was a flight, then once I landed in Denver, find a way to the hospital. If I could manage any of it, there was a good chance the soonest flight wouldn't be until tomorrow.

"I'll figure something out," I said. "Tell them I'm coming."

After ending the call, I stood in the cabin's living room, staring at my phone. JW's declaration of love seemed like a lifetime ago instead of several minutes. Real life had intruded, reminding me of the obligations and responsibilities that defined who I was now.

I grabbed my jacket and headed for the lodge, my footsteps quick on the wooden porch. Through the windows, I could see him banking the fire, preparing to close down for the night. When I knocked, he opened the door immediately, taking in my pale complexion and the phone still clutched in my hand.

"Echo? What's wrong?"

"I just got a call from work. One of our families— their little girl has taken a turn for the worse. She's been fighting for two years, and…" I couldn't finish the sentence. Even he knew what calls like this meant.

"Her parents need me," I continued, my voice steadier than I felt. "I have to get back to Colorado immediately."

"Of course," he said without hesitation. "What can I do to help?"

The unconditional offer of assistance, without questions about timing or inconvenience, reminded me why I'd fallen in love with this man, in the first place. "I was hoping to catch a flight out of Albuquerque—"

"It will take too long," he finished, understanding immediately. "By the time you drive to the airport, go through security, make connections..."

"I know, but I don't see any other option."

"I'll take you. We'll leave as soon as you're ready."

The offer took my breath away. "Are you sure?"

"I'm sure. Go pack whatever you need. I'll get the truck ready."

Five minutes later, I was throwing my belongings into my suitcase with shaking hands. The beautiful days we'd shared at Sangre Vista were ending abruptly, cut short by the demands of real life. As I zipped up my bag, I closed my eyes and took a deep breath. I couldn't allow myself to think my leaving was for the best, not when it meant a little girl was fighting for her life. But I still saw it as a sign.

A warning. I couldn't think so selfishly again. Carley's health had nothing to do with my secret, and while the devastation it would cause was nowhere near as bad as what she faced, I'd bring pain and heartache to the people I loved the most, and that wasn't something I could do. Not for JW. Not for anyone.

He was waiting on the porch when I emerged from the cabin. His truck was parked nearby, the engine already running. The ranch that had seemed so magical in daylight looked stark and remote when the moon was covered by a cloud, and I felt a pang of loss for what we were leaving behind.

"Ready?" he asked, taking my bag from my hand.

"Ready. And, JW? Thank you. For understanding, for dropping everything to help. It means more than you know."

The drive through the night was a blur of mountain highways and little conversation. JW kept us both alert with stories about building his ranch as we climbed back into Colorado. Every hour that passed brought us closer to Denver Children's Hospital, closer to a family whose world was collapsing.

"Tell me about Carley," he said as we crossed the state line, still hours from the hospital.

I found myself describing the sweet seven-year-old. How her parents had first come to Miracles of Hope when the diagnosis shattered their carefully planned life. Steve worked in construction, and Amy taught third grade—solid middle-class people who'd never imagined needing charity assistance.

"She has these enormous brown eyes," I said, staring out at the highway stretching ahead of us. "And when she smiles, even with no hair and looking so fragile, she lights up the whole room. Her parents have been incredible through everything—taking turns staying with her, keeping up with her older brother's soccer schedule, maintaining some sense of normalcy."

JW's hands tightened on the steering wheel. "How long have you been working with them?"

"Since the beginning. I was the one who helped them navigate insurance battles and connected them with housing assistance when Steve had to take unpaid leave. Amy calls me whenever she's overwhelmed." My voice caught. "I promised I'd be there if things got bad."

"And you will be."

The certainty in his voice steadied me. This was what I did—what I'd built my life around. Helping families through the worst moments imaginable, providing support when their foundations crumbled.

We reached Denver a little past midnight.

"You don't have to come in," I said when he pulled up to the front entrance.

"I'll park, and I'll wait. I'm here for whatever you or they need."

I thanked him as I fought against tears. This man, whom I'd told I needed more time after he professed his love for me, didn't waver. I didn't deserve him, but I couldn't think about that now. I had to pull myself together for Carley's sake, for her family's sake.

The pediatric oncology ward felt different in the middle of the night—quiet and still. I'd spent countless hours here, but walking these halls never got easier. The medicinal smell, the soft-soled shoes squeaking on linoleum, the muted conversations behind partially closed doors where families processed impossible news.

I found Amy standing outside Carley's door, clutching a cup of coffee that had probably gone cold hours ago. When she saw me, her composed facade crumbled.

"Echo, thank God you came."

I wrapped my arms around her, feeling the way she shook against my shoulder. "How is she?"

"Dr. Reeves says it could be hours or..." She couldn't finish the sentence. "Steve's with her now. She asked for you."

Carley's room was filled with the soft beeping of monitors and the whispered conversations of the medical staff. The little girl who'd charmed everyone at our summer picnic just weeks ago looked impossibly small in the hospital bed, surrounded by machines and tubes.

"Miss Echo!" Her voice was barely a whisper, but her eyes still held that spark I remembered.

"Hi, sweetheart. I hear you're giving everyone a scare."

She managed a smile. "Mama said you drove all night to see me."

"I did. Wouldn't want to miss visiting with my favorite girl."

Over the next several hours, I moved between Carley's room and the family lounge, helping Amy and Steve navigate conversations with doctors, coordinating with other family members, and handling the practical details that could overwhelm grieving parents. Other families filled the hallways—some celebrating small victories, others beginning journeys similar to the Wheelers'. I recognized the look in their eyes, the exhaustion that came from hoping and fearing in equal measure.

The medical staff moved through their routines with compassionate efficiency, but I could see the weight they carried too. Dr. Reeves, who'd been treating Carley since her diagnosis, had that haunted look pediatric oncologists developed after years of fighting battles they couldn't always win.

"She's comfortable," he told us during a morning update. "We're managing her pain, and she's surrounded by people who love her."

The words were kind, but we all understood what he wasn't saying directly.

As evening approached, Carley's breathing became more labored. Steve held one of her hands while Amy stroked her forehead, both parents whispering words of love and promises that they'd be okay. I stood at the foot of her bed, my professional composure intact even as my heart broke for this family.

Carley died peacefully just after sunset, with her parents' voices the last thing she heard.

The aftermath was a blur of procedures and paperwork, of helping the Wheelers make impossible decisions while their world collapsed around them. I coordinated with the funeral home they chose, connected them with our grief counseling services, and ensured they understood the charity's continued support throughout this transition.

"I don't know how we would have managed without you," Amy said as we prepared to leave the hospital hours later. "Thank you."

"Carley was an extraordinary little girl. I was honored to know her."

After the Wheelers left for home and the difficult task of telling Carley's brother what had happened, I found myself walking through the hospital corridors aimlessly. The pediatric ward had quieted again, but I couldn't bring myself to leave yet.

I took the elevator to the third floor and walked down the long hall to the hospital chapel. It was a small, non-denominational space with simple wooden pews and stained glass windows that caught the hallway lights in jeweled patterns. The room was empty, offering the kind of silence I desperately needed.

I sank into a back pew, finally allowing myself to feel the full impact of the day. Carley's death, while not unexpected, had hit me harder than I'd anticipated. Maybe because she'd been so young, or because her parents had trusted me so completely, or because losing her felt like losing all the other children I hadn't been able to save over the years.

The tears came without warning—deep, wrenching sobs that shook my entire body. All the composure I'd maintained while navigating them through their darkest day dissolved into grief I could no longer contain.

I didn't hear footsteps in the chapel doorway, wasn't aware of another presence until I felt someone settle into the pew, beside me. When I looked up through my tears, JW was there, not speaking, just present in the way I needed most.

"How did you—?" I started to ask.

"I knew you needed me, and I came."

He didn't offer platitudes about Carley being in a better place, didn't try to minimize my grief with empty reassurances. Instead, he simply sat with me while I cried, his presence a steady anchor in the storm of my emotions.

When the worst of the tears subsided, he spoke quietly. "She was lucky to have you with her."

"I couldn't save her."

"That wasn't your job. Your job was to make sure she wasn't alone, that her family had support. You did that."

"Some days, I wonder if I'm strong enough for this work," I admitted, the words escaping before I could stop them.

"Echo." He turned to face me fully. "I watched you as we drove here. Your focus was on the family from the moment you heard you needed to come. Nothing would've kept you away. That's strength."

Something in his voice and the absolute certainty of his words cracked the last of my defenses. "I'm so tired of being strong all the time."

Without hesitation, he pulled me against his chest as fresh tears began to fall. His arms encircled me completely, one hand stroking my hair while the other held me steady. For the first time in years, I allowed myself to be comforted, let someone else carry the weight I'd been bearing alone.

"That little girl showed more courage in seven years than most people find in a lifetime. She fought until the end, surrounded by love. There's beauty in that, even in grief," he murmured against my hair. "Lean on me, Echo. Let me help you carry this burden. You don't have to do it alone ever again."

His words resonated deeper than I'd expected. I thought about the secret I'd been carrying for decades, the weight of the choices I'd made when I was too young to understand their full consequences. JW spoke about not bearing burdens alone, but how could I share mine? How could I risk destroying this fragile connection we were rebuilding?

"Life is too short for fear," he continued, his voice gentle but firm. "Carley knew that, even at her young age. She didn't waste time being afraid of treatment or procedures or even dying. She just loved her family and let them love her in return."

I pulled back to look at him, seeing my own grief reflected in his eyes, but also something else—a deep understanding of loss and the preciousness of time.

"JW, I…" I shook my head, unable to push him away again.

"We've already lost thirty years. Echo. We can't get those back, but we don't have to waste whatever time we have left." His hands framed my face, thumbs brushing away tears. "Our love has endured through all the time we've been apart. I know you love me just as much as I love you. We can do this. We can get past the pain and hurt and uncertainty."

The chapel fell silent around us, broken only by the distant sounds of hospital activity beyond the doors. In this quiet sanctuary, surrounded by the echoes of others' prayers and hopes, I felt something shift inside me.

"You're right. I never stopped loving you," I whispered, the admission torn from someplace deep and hidden. "Even when I hated you for leaving, even when I convinced myself I'd moved on—I never stopped."

His intake of breath was sharp, his eyes searching mine. "Maya—"

"I was so angry when you came back. Terrified of feeling everything again, of risking the life I'd built on the assumption that you were gone forever." The words came faster now, as if Carley's death had broken something open that had been sealed too long. "But watching her family today, seeing how they loved each other even knowing it would end—maybe the risk is worth it."

JW's forehead touched mine, his eyes closing as if in prayer. "It is. I believe that with all my heart."

"I want to see what we could be now, as the people we've become." My voice grew stronger with each word. "I want to try again. To give us a chance."

When he kissed me, it tasted of tears but also of the sweetness of new beginnings. In the hospital chapel, surrounded by the weight of loss and the fragility of life, I let him in and knew I could never let him go again.

"So what happens now?" I asked, still wrapped in his arms.

"Now, we take each day as it comes. No more wasted time."

I nodded, holding tight to his words and to him. Praying it could be that simple.

19

JW

The drive back to Crested Butte from Denver stretched through the early morning hours, both of us emotionally drained from Carley's death, but somehow lighter too. Echo dozed while I navigated the mountain highways, her hand resting in mine on the console—a simple touch that felt like everything.

We'd crossed a threshold in that hospital chapel. After thirty years of separation and weeks of careful dancing around each other, we'd finally admitted what we both knew. We still loved each other, and we weren't going to waste any more time pretending otherwise.

"Come inside," Echo said as we pulled into her driveway. "I need coffee, and we should talk."

Her house was exactly what I'd imagined—cozy and welcoming, with books stacked on tables and photographs covering the mantle. It felt like her, warm and thoughtful. She moved around the kitchen, making coffee while I took in the space that had been her sanctuary all these years.

"So we're really doing this," she said, setting mugs between us. Not a question.

"We are." I reached across the table for her hand. "The arrangements we've discussed—me here most of the time, trips to Sangre Vista when needed—will that work for you?"

"It will. You'll be busy at Roaring Fork when we're here. Either working or with your grandchildren." She smiled and winked, then her expression turned serious. "My work will have its emergencies, like yesterday."

"And I'll drive you wherever you need to go," I said. "You won't face any of it alone again, Echo."

The look of relief that spread across her face was worth every mile, every tank of gas, every sleepless night.

"You should get some rest," I said, standing to leave.

"Oh, um, right." She stood too and walked me to the door.

"Before I go, there's something I need." I cupped her cheek and wound my other arm around her waist.

Echo's eyes met mine, and in them, I saw the same desire I felt. The same heated look I remembered from years ago. I wanted this woman with every breath I took, but our reunion was still fragile. She'd given in and agreed to try again, but if I pushed too hard, I risked her changing her mind.

I kissed her long, slow, and deep, loving the feeling of her breasts crushed against my chest when I pulled her closer so she could feel how hard I was for her.

"Do you have to leave?" she asked.

"Not if you want me to stay."

"I do." She led me toward the back of the house, to her bedroom.

When we reached the threshold, I stopped. "Echo…"

She stopped too. "If I misunderstood—"

I silenced her with another kiss that was full of passion, and heat, and promise. "You didn't. I just want to make sure you really want this."

She half smiled. "Isn't it obvious?"

I smiled too. "Perhaps not as obvious as my desire for you."

"JW, I want this. More than anything. Now that the door has opened, I can't close it. I burn for you, JW."

The air was thick with anticipation, a silent symphony of heartbeats echoing through the room when we walked in. Her bedroom was bathed in afternoon sunlight. The scent of lavender filled the air, a soft, lingering whisper of tranquility amidst the storm of emotions that threatened to overwhelm me.

"Come here," I said, standing at the end of the bed, waiting to see if she'd respond to me the way she used to.

Echo stood in front of me, arms at her sides. I unfastened the buttons of her shirt and spread it open. Her bra, pink and lacy, was too much of a temptation. I leaned forward, snaked my arm around her waist again, then ran my tongue along the seam that covered her breasts. When her knees buckled, I pulled her closer, holding her weight with mine, then covered one nipple with my mouth, sucking through the sheer fabric.

"JW, please," she mewled.

Still holding her with one arm, I unfastened the clasp of her bra, then moved each strap from her shoulders. She shimmied it from her body, then reached for the button of her jeans.

"Let me," I pleaded, falling to my knees. With each one I unfastened, my tongue followed as, little by little, her naked flesh was exposed. I pulled them down her legs, then took in the sight of her. Echo was a vision of desire and nostalgia. Her expression that I'd drowned in so many times before held a mix of trepidation and longing, and I could see the pulse at the base of her throat, a steady rhythm that matched the beat of my own heart.

I stood and traced the outline of her jaw, her neck, down her sternum. My weathered hand was rough against her soft skin that was hot with her desire.

"You are so beautiful, Echo," I murmured, my voice a low growl. "You take my breath away."

She smiled, soft but sad. "You always did know what to say to make me want you more," she whispered.

"Lie on the bed for me."

Her breath hitched as my hand moved lower, and I could see the goosebumps rise in the wake of my touch.

My thumb brushed over the pebble-hard nipple I'd had in my mouth, pinching it gently, just enough to make her gasp and her back arch off the bed. "I never meant to hurt you, Echo," I said, spreading her legs to rest between them.

"I know," she whispered, her hands reaching up to pull my head down to hers. Our lips met in a clash of teeth and tongue, a desperate, hungry kiss that left us both panting.

Reaching one hand between us, my fingers brushed through the soft curls at the apex of her thighs.

I could feel her heat and the dampness that betrayed her arousal. I slipped a finger inside and pressed my thumb against her clit. She moaned into my mouth, and her eyes fluttered shut.

"God, you're so wet. So ready for me."

I added another finger, stretching her, preparing her. Her muscles clenched around me, and her hips moved in time with my thrusts. I added a third finger, and she cried out, her body tensing as I pressed against her flesh.

"That's it, baby," I whispered.

I could feel her body relaxing, opening up to me, thrusting back with increasing urgency. When I curled my fingers, pressing against her flesh, she let out a low moan and her head rocked from side to side.

"JW!" Her eyes met mine. "I need you. *Please.*"

The words sent a jolt of electricity coursing through me.

I withdrew my fingers, making her whimper at the loss. But her protest turned into a moan of pleasure as I stood, pulled my shirt over my head, unbuckled my belt, pushed down my pants, then stood before her.

"Echo, I haven't been with anyone for a very long time—"

"Neither have I." She reached for my cock and wrapped her fingers around it, positioning it at her opening.

My heart pounded in my chest. "Echo," I whispered, my voice so raw with emotion I couldn't say what I desperately wanted to.

She reached up with her free hand and cupped my face. "Make love to me, JW," she whispered. "Make me yours again."

I didn't need to be told twice. She released me, and I surged forward, my hips slamming against hers, burying myself deep inside her. We both let out a gasp, our bodies tensing at the sudden intrusion.

"You feel so good," I groaned, my hips already moving, my cock sliding in and out of her with slow, deliberate thrusts. "So hot and tight. Just like I remember, baby," I grunted. My hands gripped her hips so I could go deeper.

"Harder, JW. I want to feel you. All of you."

I obliged, my thrusts becoming more urgent, more demanding. The sound of our flesh meeting filled the room.

I leaned down, capturing one of her nipples in my mouth and swirling it with my tongue.

A low moan escaped Echo's lips as I suckled her, and her fingers tangled in the silver strands of my hair, pulling me closer. "Don't stop," she pleaded.

My hands dropped from her hips to grip her thighs, spreading her wider for my invasion. I thrust into her harder and faster. The bed creaked beneath us, and the headboard knocked against the wall.

Echo's eyes were closed, her head thrown back, and her mouth open in a silent cry of pleasure. Her breasts bounced with each thrust, her nipples hard and aching for more. I took the other into my mouth again, my teeth grazing the sensitive peak, then sucked hard as my hips moved in a relentless rhythm that matched the urgent need coursing through my veins. I could feel her body tensing, her muscles clenching around me, her breath coming in short, sharp gasps.

"JW," she cried out, her hips meeting my thrusts with wild abandon. "God, don't stop."

I couldn't have, even if she'd wanted me to. I was a man possessed, driven by the need to claim her, to mark her, to make her mine again. I could taste her sweat, feel her heat, hear her cries of pleasure.

Each push brought me closer to the edge, to the point of no return. I wanted to hold on, to drag out the moment, but Echo's body was tightening around me, and her moans were becoming louder, more demanding.

"Harder. I need…I need…"

I obliged without her saying the words. My hips moved like a piston, my cock slamming into her with bruising force. Her body trembled, making me want to send her over, to watch those beautiful eyes roll back in her head as she came undone beneath me.

I reached between us, my fingers finding her sensitive nub swollen. I rubbed it in time with my thrusts.

Echo let out a cry, and her body convulsed as a powerful orgasm tore through her. "JW," she shouted, her nails raking down my back again.

"Again," I demanded.

She quivered, and I wanted to savor every second of this, but her mewls of pleasure were like a burning match to my self-control.

"You feel so damn good, Echo." I shifted my hips, angling my cock to hit that spot deep inside her, the one that made her gasp and writhe. "Is this what you want, baby?" I thrust into her harder, deeper, my cock slamming against her cervix. "Tell me you want more."

"Yes," she moaned through clenched teeth. "God, yes. More."

I pulled back, almost all the way out, before slamming into her again, my hips moving in a relentless, punishing rhythm.

"You like that, don't you, baby?" I growled. "You like feeling my cock deep inside you, filling you up, making you mine."

"Yes. You know I do." Echo nodded, her breath coming in short, sharp gasps.

She wrapped her legs around my waist, and her heels dug into my ass, urging me on. "Please," she panted.

I didn't need further encouragement. My fingers dug into her soft flesh as I held her still and pounded into her.

"That's it, baby," I groaned, my voice thick with lust and desire. "Take all of me."

Echo nodded, her eyes locked onto mine, and her pussy gripped my cock like a vice. "Yes," she moaned, her voice ragged. "I want all of you. I never stopped wanting you."

I knew she was close, could feel her tension building. When I made her come for the second time, she convulsed around my cock and her screams filled the room. But it wasn't enough. I needed more. I needed everything, and I took it, roaring her name—Maya, not Echo—as my release left me breathless and sated.

I shifted and lay beside her. Our bodies were covered in a sheen of sweat as we both struggled to catch our breath.

"I'm sorry for calling you Maya," I said a few minutes later.

"It's okay."

"Can I ask what made you decide to go by Echo instead?"

"There was a time in my life when I wanted to be someone very different from the girl you knew. I needed a fresh start, so I left Maya behind."

"I need you to know that I—"

"Shh." She pressed her fingers against my lips. "Being with you again was perfect, JW. Just as incredible as I remembered."

Sex between us had always been wild and passionate. Even the first time, when neither of us knew what we were doing, our bodies innately figured it out. I'd never experienced anything close to it with the few other women I'd been with.

No one was like Echo. No one would ever be. This time, I wouldn't be so foolish as to let her go. She told me to make her mine again, and I did. Just like she'd made me hers.

The next few weeks fell into a flow that felt surprisingly natural. I split my time between Echo's house and the guest cabin at Roaring Fork, slowly integrating myself into her daily life while helping at the Roaring Fork.

Echo threw herself back into her work with renewed energy, and I found myself accompanying her to site visits and family meetings when she wanted the support. Watching her with grieving families, seeing how she balanced compassion with practical help, only deepened my respect for the woman she'd become.

One evening in mid-September, we were walking along the Slate River after dinner when certainty hit me like lightning.

"Echo," I said, stopping on the path.

She turned, immediately picking up on the change in my tone. "What is it?"

I'd been carrying the small box for a week, waiting for the perfect moment. But standing here, in the place where we'd first confronted our past, where she'd fled from me and later let me explain, I realized there was no moment more perfect than this.

"I love you," I said, dropping to one knee.

Her hands flew to her mouth. "JW—"

"I've loved you for thirty years. I wasted three decades, believing my obligations were more important than my happiness, than our happiness." I pulled out the band with a simple solitaire. "I don't want to waste another day. Marry me, Echo."

Tears streamed down her face as she looked from it to my face and back again. "Yes," she whispered. "Yes, of course, yes."

My hands shook as I slipped the ring onto her finger. When I stood, she launched herself into my arms, kissing me with the same joy I felt.

"I can't believe this is real," she said against my lips.

"It's real. We're real." I kissed her again and again. Marveling at feeling whole in a way I hadn't felt since the night before my mother and I got in my truck and drove away from Crested Butte, not knowing if we'd ever return. "I don't want to wait, my love. I've waited too long already."

"When?" she asked.

"As soon as possible. I'd marry you tomorrow if I could. Today, if you'd agree."

"I don't want to delay or rush, but I want to celebrate our love with our families and friends. I want Kingston to be there. Is that okay?"

"As long as I can kiss you, touch you, and feel your naked body next to mine, we'll already be married in my mind. When it becomes official, it won't change anything."

"It can be a simple ceremony…"

Over the following days, we discovered that "simple" was relative when it came to weddings. Echo had friends and colleagues who'd want to attend. I had the entire Wheaton clan plus my staff from Sangre Vista. Simple could still mean fifty people.

"Where should we have it?" Echo asked one evening as we sat in her living room.

"Wherever you want."

"That's not helpful." She nudged me with her elbow. "I'm serious. This is important."

I'd been thinking about it, actually. "What about Roaring Fork Ranch?"

Her eyebrows rose. "Really?"

"Unless you'd prefer somewhere else."

Echo was quiet for a moment, considering. "It would be perfect, JW." She leaned up to kiss me, and I tasted happiness on her lips. "I love the idea, but we have to check with Flynn and her brothers. They may not want us taking over their ranch for a day."

I laughed. "Echo, they've been plotting to get us together since the Fourth of July, Flynn especially."

The next day, we drove out to Roaring Fork to present our idea. Flynn took one look at Echo's ring, and her eyes filled with tears.

"Oh, this is perfect!" she said, pulling us both into a hug. "Getting married here at the ranch will be magical. When are you thinking?"

"Whatever's practical," I said. "But as soon as possible."

"How many people do you anticipate inviting?"

"Maybe fifty," Echo said.

"The dining hall can easily hold that many. If the weather is nice, the ceremony could be outside…"

Flynn and Echo's conversation faded into the background as I looked around the room where I'd last seen Patricia alive. My mom and I had risked one last visit to say goodbye. But today, I could feel her presence. I could almost hear her voice, saying how happy she was for us. While my goal had been to complete my promise to her, to ensure her kids were happy and living full lives, I realized now that Flynn's journey hadn't been the last. Mine was.

20

Echo

I sat across from my older sister, Dawn, at our favorite corner table in McGill's. She studied me with the intensity that had driven me crazy as a child, but now felt like an interrogation.

"You're glowing," she said, her smile warm but searching. "I haven't seen you this happy in…well, maybe ever."

My hands trembled around my coffee cup as I attempted a smile. "Not for a very long time anyway."

"JW makes you happy."

It wasn't a question, but I nodded anyway. "He does. More than I thought possible."

When she reached across the table and squeezed my hand, I resisted the urge to pull away. "I'm so glad you two found your way back to each other. When you told me he'd returned, I wasn't sure what to think. But seeing you now…"

"What?" The word came out sharper than I'd intended.

Dawn's eyes flared. "You look like yourself again. The person you were before everything went sideways all those years ago."

"That feels like a lifetime ago," I murmured.

"It was." Her tone grew more serious, and I knew what was coming. "Echo, does JW know? About what happened after he left?"

My stomach clenched. I'd been dreading the question even though I was certain it was coming.

"There's no reason he needs to know." The words sounded hollow even to my own ears. "That's all in the past. The choices I made then were the best for everyone."

Dawn studied my expression with a penetrating gaze. I looked away, unable to meet her scrutiny.

"If you're sure," she finally said, but doubt colored her words.

"I am. We can all continue to live our lives. What matters is what we have now." The response tasted like ash.

Relief flickered across my sister's face, followed by genuine excitement that made my chest ache with guilt. "Then, I'm happy for you. Truly. You deserve this, Echo. You deserve love and joy and all the good things life has to offer."

Did I? Did I deserve happiness built on deception? The knot in my chest tightened until I could barely breathe.

"Thank you," I managed.

Dawn launched into enthusiastic questions about the ceremony, but her words seemed to come from far away. I answered automatically, mechanically, while my mind spiraled through the same torturous loop it had been trapped in for days.

Tell him. Don't tell him. Ruin everything. Save everyone.

"Echo?" Dawn's words cut through my panic. "I asked about the flowers."

"Flowers?" I blinked, trying to focus. "Oh. Yes. Flynn's handling everything."

Lines appeared between Dawn's brows. "Are you feeling all right? You seem distracted."

"Just busy." The lies came easier now, polished by repetition. "The end of the fiscal year always brings stress."

But even as I said it, I could see she wasn't convinced. My sister knew me too well, had seen me through too much.

We finished breakfast without her asking any more questions, but I could feel her worried gaze following me as I left the restaurant. My hands shook as I started my car, and I had to sit for several minutes before I trusted myself to drive.

The office felt like a refuge until I realized it wasn't. The grant applications on my desk might as well have been written in a foreign language. I read the same paragraph five times before giving up and moving to the next file.

My phone rang, startling me so badly that I knocked over my coffee mug.

"Echo West," I answered, grabbing napkins to clean up the mess.

"Mrs. West, this is Dr. Robbins from Children's Hospital. We discussed the Patterson family last week?"

I stared at my calendar, panic rising. The Patterson family. Eight-year-old daughter with brain cancer. I was supposed to have processed their emergency assistance request yesterday.

"Yes, of course. I'm so sorry—I've been reviewing their file and should have the paperwork completed by—"

"They were discharged yesterday," she interrupted gently. "The family was counting on our help with the hotel costs."

The room tilted sideways. I'd forgotten. Completely forgotten a family in crisis, because I couldn't stop obsessing over my own problems.

"I'm so sorry. Let me call them right away, and—"

"It's all right. We managed to find alternative funding. But, Echo, this isn't like you."

After I hung up, I sat staring at the phone, revulsion washing through me. This was exactly what I'd sworn would never happen. My personal life was affecting my work, and families were paying the price.

I tried to focus for the rest of the morning, but my concentration was shattered. Every phone call felt like navigating through fog. Every decision required enormous effort. By lunch, Melanie had knocked on my door three times with questions about things I was supposed to take care of.

"Echo, I think you should go home," she said during her third visit, her tone gentle but firm. "You're clearly not well."

"I'm fine," I protested, but even I could hear how unconvincing I sounded.

"When was the last time you ate? You look pale."

I couldn't remember eating breakfast, despite sitting through an entire meal with Dawn. My stomach felt hollow, but the thought of food made me nauseous.

"Maybe you're right," I admitted.

Instead of going home, I drove aimlessly through the mountains, taking back roads that led nowhere. The autumn colors that had seemed so beautiful last week had now faded into dullness.

I pulled over when my phone buzzed with a text from JW. *How's your day going? Thinking of you.*

I stared at the message until the words blurred. How could I respond? That I was falling apart? That I was lying to everyone, including myself? That I was about to destroy the best thing that had ever happened to me?

Good day. See you tonight, I typed back.

That evening, I stood outside JW's cabin for several minutes before knocking, trying to compose myself.

The warm light spilling from his windows, the smoke curling from his chimney—it all looked like a promise of happiness I didn't deserve.

"There's my beautiful bride-to-be," he said when he opened the door, his expression lighting up in a way that usually filled my heart.

I attempted a smile, but it felt like wearing a mask that might crack at any moment. "Hi."

He pulled me into his arms, and for a moment, I let myself sink into his warmth. But even his embrace couldn't quiet the chaos in my head.

"You seem tired," he said.

"Long day at work." Another lie. They were coming so easily now.

During dinner, I picked at the meal he'd prepared, unable to taste anything through my mounting panic. JW glanced at me with growing concern, and I could see him struggling with whether to push.

"Echo, you've barely touched your food."

"I'm just not very hungry." I made myself take a bite, though it felt like swallowing sawdust.

"Are you getting sick? You look pale."

"I'm fine." The sharp edge in my tone surprised us both.

JW set down his fork. "What's really going on? And please don't say work again. This is more than that."

My heart pounded so hard I was sure he could hear it. "I told you, I'm fine."

"No, you're not." His words were gentle but insistent. "You've been distant lately. Distracted. You jump every time your phone rings, you barely eat, and you look like you haven't slept in days."

Because I hadn't. Every night brought the same torment—lying awake, staring at the ceiling, rehearsing confessions I'd never have the courage to make.

"It's just prewedding nerves," I said weakly.

"Is it?" He leaned forward, searching my expression. "Because if you're having second thoughts, if you don't want to marry me—"

"No!" The word exploded out of me. "I want to marry you more than anything. That's the problem."

JW's brow furrowed. "I don't understand."

Neither did I. How could I explain that loving him was destroying me? That every day we spent together made the weight of my secret heavier?

"I just want everything to be perfect," I said, hating myself for the continued deception.

But JW wasn't buying it anymore. I could see the worry in his expression, the way he was trying to piece together whatever was happening to me.

"Echo, whatever's troubling you, we can work through it together. You don't have to carry it alone."

His kindness was like salt in a wound. Here was this incredible man, offering to share my burdens, and I couldn't even tell him what they were.

"I know," I whispered, looking away.

The rest of the evening passed in strained silence. JW tried to engage me in conversation, but my responses were monosyllabic, distracted. I could feel him pulling back, hurt by my distance but not knowing how to bridge it.

When I left that night, his goodbye was subdued. "Get some rest," he said, kissing my forehead.

I drove home through empty streets, tears blurring my vision. At home, I sat in my dark living room, not bothering to turn on the lights, and faced the reality I'd been avoiding.

I was destroying everything. My work was suffering. JW was suffering. I was barely holding myself together, and in five days, I was supposed to stand up in front of everyone and promise to share my life with a man I was already lying to.

The next three days blurred together in a haze of panic and artificial smiles. Flynn bustled around, making the final preparations, her excitement palpable while I moved through the motions like a ghost. During our last planning meeting, she stopped mid-sentence to stare at me.

"Echo, are you all right? You look terrible."

"Thank you," I said dryly, but there was no humor in it.

"I'm serious. Should we call a doctor? You might be coming down with something."

"I'm fine. Just tired."

"No. This isn't excitement or nerves. Something else is going on."

I attempted another smile. "It's nothing I can't handle."

The lie sat heavy between us, and I could see Flynn filing away her concerns for later discussion.

The night before the ceremony, we gathered at the ranch for the rehearsal. The evening should have been joyful—family and friends coming together to celebrate love and new beginnings. Instead, I felt like I was moving through quicksand, every step requiring enormous effort.

JW barely left my side, his protective instincts clearly triggered by whatever he was seeing in my behavior. But his presence, instead of comforting me, only increased my agitation.

During the mock ceremony, when we were supposed to exchange practice vows, I froze completely. The words stuck in my throat, and I stood there, opening and closing my mouth like a fish out of water.

"It's all right," Flynn said quickly, covering for me. "We'll save the real magic for tomorrow."

But JW's eyes never left mine, and I could see the questions there, the growing alarm.

After everyone else dispersed to their rooms or homes, JW and I lingered in the ranch house's main room. Tomorrow, we would be married. I'd promise to love and honor and be honest with this man while keeping the biggest secret of my life from him.

"Would you like me to drive you home?" he asked carefully, like he was speaking to something fragile that might break.

"No, I can manage," I responded, but my feet wouldn't move.

We stood in awkward silence, and I could feel him trying to read my mood, trying to understand what was happening between us.

"Echo, whatever's wrong, we can fix it. But you have to tell me what it is."

The opening I'd been both longing for and dreading. My heart hammered against my ribs as I looked at him—this man who loved me, who trusted me, who deserved so much better than my lies of omission.

"JW," I began, my words barely a whisper.

"Yes?"

The truth was right there, hovering on my lips. The revelation that would either free us or destroy us completely. My mouth opened and closed several times as I struggled to find the courage.

"There's something I need to tell you," I finally managed, my voice shaking. "Something I should have told you weeks ago."

His body went very still, focused on me with an intensity that made me want to run. "What is it?"

"A few days after you left, I discovered I was pregnant—" My words broke, and I had to take a shuddering breath.

Before I could speak again, the front door burst open, interrupting my confession. Kingston walked in, followed by a woman with a bright smile, someone I hadn't expected to see tonight.

My blood turned to ice as recognition hit. The words I'd been about to speak died in my throat, replaced by a shock so complete it left me speechless.

This couldn't be happening. Not tonight. Not now. Not when I'd finally found the courage to tell JW the truth myself.

21

JW

Earlier, I'd been elated. Tomorrow, I would marry the woman I'd loved for thirty years, surrounded by the family that had welcomed me as their own. The rehearsal had gone perfectly, Flynn had outdone herself with the preparations, and everything was coming together beautifully.

The ranch house's dining room glowed with candlelight and autumn wildflowers. Conversation flowed easily around the long wooden table as family and friends celebrated our upcoming union. I should have been savoring every moment, storing up memories of this perfect evening.

Instead, my attention kept drifting to the woman beside me.

Echo was doing her best to hide her anxiety, but I could see it in the way she gripped her fork, how she flinched when people spoke to her. It had been getting worse as our wedding day approached, and tonight, it was impossible to ignore.

She sat rigidly in her chair, cutting her food into pieces she never brought to her mouth. Her responses to the conversation came after long pauses, like she was translating from another language. When Flynn asked about her dress, Echo stared blankly for several seconds before remembering to answer.

The transformation was jarring. The confident woman who ran a major charity, who could comfort grieving families in their darkest hours, had been replaced by someone who seemed to be holding herself together through sheer will.

"JW, you're getting yourself quite a woman," Holt said, raising his glass. "Echo's been a blessing to our family. She helped us navigate Luna's treatment when we didn't know up from down."

I forced a smile and squeezed Echo's hand. Her fingers were ice cold despite the warm room.

"Second chances don't come often," Buck said, his tone growing serious. "Most of us don't get to reclaim something we lost. When Patricia created that trust, I don't think she could have imagined it would lead to moments like this."

Porter nodded. "The trust taught me that running from love only makes you more lost. Finding Cici again, building something real with her—that's what saved me."

"Marriage changes everything," said Cord, looking at his wife with obvious affection. "In the best way. You realize you're not facing life alone anymore. Every burden gets lighter when there's someone willing to share it."

I watched Echo's face tighten at the siblings' words about sharing burdens.

Holt leaned forward. "Building a family together—there's nothing like it. Even when it's complicated, even when the past throws curveballs, you figure it out together."

"What matters is that you found each other again," Buck added. "After all these years, after everything that kept you apart, that's pretty remarkable. Love like yours doesn't die—it just waits."

I listened to the men who had become like sons to me speak, grateful for their acceptance and wisdom. Each had overcome their own obstacles to find happiness, and while they meant to bring comfort, their words seemed to agitate Echo further.

Her breathing had grown shallow, and she kept glancing toward the door like she was calculating escape routes. When Luna laughed at something Keltie said, Echo jumped as if she'd been struck.

"Echo," I said softly, leaning closer so our conversation wouldn't carry. "Are you feeling all right?"

She turned to me with eyes that looked haunted. "I'm fine."

But she wasn't fine. The strain in her voice made my chest tighten with worry.

I tried different approaches throughout the evening. When she pushed the food around her plate without eating, I suggested we step outside for fresh air. She declined. When her hands trembled while reaching for her water glass, I covered them with mine, trying to warm them. She pulled away. When the conversation grew loud and animated, making her startle repeatedly, I suggested we find a quieter spot. She shook her head.

Nothing I offered seemed to help. If anything, my attempts to comfort her only seemed to increase her distress.

As the evening wore on, Echo's mood worsened. Dark circles shadowed her eyes, more pronounced in the candlelight. Her skin had taken on a grayish pallor that concerned me. She'd lost weight over the past week—weight she couldn't afford to lose—and tonight, her clothes hung loose on her frame.

Flynn noticed too. I caught her studying Echo with the same worried expression I probably wore. When Echo excused herself to use the restroom, Flynn followed. They returned several minutes later, but Echo looked even more strained than before.

As guests began to disperse and Flynn started clearing the dishes, the ranch house grew quieter. Echo and I remained in the main room while the last conversations faded and car doors slammed outside.

She stood by the window overlooking the dark mountains, her reflection ghosted in the glass. Her posture spoke of defeat, like she was carrying a weight too heavy to manage.

The silence stretched between us until it became unbearable. Tomorrow, we were supposed to stand before everyone and promise to share our lives. But right now, the woman I loved felt like a stranger.

"Echo, please talk to me."

She turned from the window, and what I saw in her expression made my blood run cold. Not just anxiety or nerves, but something closer to despair.

"We need to talk," she said, her voice barely above a whisper.

My gut clenched with her words. The way she said them, the finality in her tone—she was calling off the wedding. After everything we'd been through, after finding each other again, she was going to end it.

My throat constricted, making it difficult to speak. "Of course."

She moved to the sofa, perching on the edge like she might bolt at any moment. I sat beside her, close enough to offer comfort but far enough to give her space.

"I can't marry you until I tell you something," she began, her words shaking. "Something I should have told you weeks ago."

I waited, my heart hammering against my ribs as she struggled to speak. She wrapped her arms around herself as tears spilled over onto her cheeks.

The silence stretched until I wondered if she'd lost her nerve entirely. When she finally spoke, her voice was so quiet I had to lean forward to hear her.

"A few days after you left, I discovered I was pregnant…"

The words landed like stones in still water, sending ripples through everything I thought I knew. Pregnant. She'd been carrying my child when I fled to Crested Butte, abandoning her to face an unplanned pregnancy alone.

My mind began connecting the dots with sickening clarity. The timeline, the age—*Bridger must be my son.* That quiet, talented young man who'd impressed me with his work ethic and musical ability was my child. All these months, I'd been getting to know him without realizing I was meeting my own flesh and blood.

The weight of that realization was still settling over me, the magnitude of what I'd missed, what Echo had endured alone, when there was a knock at the door.

"JW? Mom? You in here?" Bridger's voice carried through the heavy wood.

We both froze, staring at each other across the emotional chasm that had opened between us. I was about to tell her I thought I knew what she was trying to say when the door opened.

Bridger walked in, followed by a woman I'd never seen before. My breath caught in my throat as I took in her features.

She looked exactly like my mother had when she was younger—the same dark hair styled in loose waves, the same delicate bone structure, even the same graceful way of moving. But this wasn't just a resemblance. She had my eyes, the same green that looked back at me from mirrors. My jawline, strong and defined. The same slight cleft in her chin that had been passed down through generations of Rookers.

My daughter. This was my daughter.

Blood rushed in my ears as bewilderment washed over me. I heard the woman say, "As soon as Bridger told me about the wedding, I booked a flight, but I almost didn't make it in time to see Aunt Echo get married!"

She hurried across the room, her face glowing with happiness. "I'm so excited for you! Seeing you find love again—it's beyond wonderful!"

I watched Echo's face drain of all color, saw her body go rigid as she stared at the newcomer. Raw fear radiated from her every muscle as she seemed to shrink in on herself.

The woman grabbed Echo's hands, bouncing slightly with enthusiasm. "I know it's last minute, but I couldn't miss this." She turned toward me with expectant eyes. "Aunt Echo, introduce me to your fiancé!"

Echo's mouth opened and closed soundlessly. Her breathing became rapid and shallow, like she was having a panic attack.

"I—I can't—" she stammered, rushing toward the door. "I can't do this."

She fled the house, leaving the three of us in stunned silence.

The young woman looked confused and hurt, glancing between the door Echo had disappeared through and me. Bridger's expression was apologetic and concerned.

He stepped forward, filling the uncomfortable silence. "JW, this is my cousin, Gisela."

I shook her hand automatically, my thoughts spinning as I struggled to process what I was seeing.

"How nice it is to meet you," I managed, though my voice sounded distant to my own ears.

Gisela's smile faltered. "Did I say something wrong? I didn't mean to upset her."

"She's been nervous about the wedding," Bridger said, though his furrowed brow suggested he was as confused as his cousin.

My mind reeled with questions I couldn't begin to voice. "Forgive me, but I must find Echo."

I bolted through the front door, desperate to understand what was happening, but terrified of what other revelations awaited.

22

Echo

I raced out of the ranch house, my feet barely touching the wooden porch steps as I fled toward my car. I knew they all had questions, but I couldn't stop, couldn't turn around.

My hands shook so violently that I could barely get the key in the ignition. When the engine finally turned over, I pressed the accelerator harder than I should have, gravel spraying behind me as I tore down the ranch's long driveway. Through panicked sobs that blurred my vision, I managed to navigate the winding mountain roads back to town, my entire body trembling with the magnitude of what had just happened.

The secret I'd carried for nearly thirty years had just walked through the door, calling me Aunt Echo in front of the man I was supposed to marry tomorrow. The daughter I'd given birth to but could never claim. The child I'd watched from a distance, knowing she was mine but never able to tell her.

And JW had seen it. The recognition in his eyes when he'd looked at Gisela—he'd seen his own features reflected in her just as clearly as I saw them every day since she was born. There was no hiding it now. No pretending.

I barely remembered parking in my driveway or fumbling with my house keys. Once inside, I collapsed on my sofa and wept harder than I had since the day I'd placed my newborn daughter in Dawn's care. I'd known it was for the best, but that I'd never hear her call me Mommy tore at my heart.

How could I have been so naive? How could I have thought I could marry JW without him ever knowing about Gisela? That I could build a life with him on a foundation of subterfuge? The weight of my lies of omission came crashing down on me, and I felt like I was drowning.

I thought about the wedding dress hanging in my closet, the flowers Flynn had arranged, the cake that would feed fifty guests tomorrow afternoon. I thought about the vows I'd written, promising to share my life honestly with the man I cherished. What a joke that was. What a terrible, cruel joke.

The knock at my door came sooner than I'd expected, but I knew it would come. I'd known JW wouldn't let me run without a fight, not after what he'd just witnessed.

"Echo, please let me in."

I stared at the door, knowing he had a key. I'd given it to him when we decided we wanted to share our lives completely. But I understood why he wasn't using it— he wanted me to let him in metaphorically as much as literally. He was giving me the choice, the control I'd lost the moment Gisela walked into that room.

For a long moment, I considered not answering. Considered letting him think I wasn't home, that I'd fled somewhere he couldn't find me. But where would I go? And what would be the point? The truth was out now, whether I wanted to face it or not.

I pulled the door open with trembling hands, not knowing what to expect. My appearance was disheveled, my carefully applied makeup completely destroyed. I was still shaking, unable to speak through the sobs that wouldn't stop.

What shocked me was that JW immediately drew me close. No questions, no demands for explanation, no anger or accusation. Just his strong embrace wrapping around me, holding me against his chest as if he could shield me from the storm tearing through me.

I struggled against him at first, trying to push him away. I didn't deserve his comfort. I didn't deserve his kindness. I'd lied to him, built our entire relationship on a foundation of deception. But he held me tighter, one hand stroking my hair, the other rubbing soothing circles on my back.

"I'm so sorry," he whispered into my hair, his own voice thick with pain. "I'm so sorry I left you."

His words broke something open inside me, and I collapsed against him completely, letting him support my weight as fresh waves of grief shook my body. He lifted me in his arms and carried me down the hall to the bedroom, rested my body on the bed gently, then lay beside me, pulling me as close as he could.

He didn't immediately ask for an explanation, but I knew I owed him one. Like when he'd confessed to me why he left all those years ago, baring his soul and sharing his deepest pain, I owed him the same courtesy. The truth, all of it, no matter how much it hurt to say the words out loud.

I leaned back and looked into his eyes. "You need to know the truth."

"Eventually, I'd like to, but it doesn't have to be now."

"It does." I took a deep breath and let it out slowly. "Like I said at the ranch," I began, my voice breaking with every word, "a few days after you left, I discovered I was pregnant."

JW's hold on me tightened, but he didn't speak. He just held me, letting me find the strength to continue.

"I was nineteen years old and lost. I had no idea what to do, no one to turn to. You were gone without a trace, and I had no idea how to find you." The memories came flooding back with painful clarity, as vivid as if they'd happened yesterday.

"I stayed in my room for two days after taking that pregnancy test, too terrified to tell anyone. But my mother knew something was wrong. She'd always been able to read me, and she kept pressing me until I couldn't hide it anymore."

I pulled back slightly to look at JW's expression, needing to see his reaction. "I came out of my room with the test still in my hand, and she was waiting for me in the hallway. The moment she saw my appearance, she knew."

"What did she say?"

"She was furious. Started yelling about how I'd ruined my life, how I'd destroyed any chance of a decent future. She said my father would never accept this disgrace, that our family's reputation would be destroyed."

I took a shaky breath before continuing. "Then she told me that before my father found out, I had to terminate the pregnancy. That it was the only way to fix what I'd done."

I felt JW stiffen against me, and I knew he was thinking about the similarities—this was exactly the situation that had forced him, his mother, and Patricia to flee East Aurora all those years ago. History almost repeating itself in the most painful way possible.

"We argued for what felt like hours," I continued. "I kept telling her I couldn't do it, wouldn't do it. That I couldn't end my baby's life, your baby's life, no matter what the consequences were. That's when my father walked in."

JW's hand found mine, squeezing gently. "He heard everything?"

"He heard me say I was pregnant and that I refused to get an abortion. I'll never forget the way his mouth fell open, then his features twisted with revulsion. Like

I was something filthy he'd found on the bottom of his shoe." I wiped my eyes with the back of my hand. "He didn't say a word at first. Just stared at me. Then he told me to pack my things and get out of his house. Said I was no daughter of his."

"Echo," JW whispered, anguish evident in his tone.

"I threw whatever I could fit into a suitcase and drove to where my sister, Dawn, lived with her husband, Mark, about an hour away. I could barely get the words out to explain what had happened."

The memory of that night was still crystal clear. Dawn opening the door to find me sobbing on her doorstep, pregnant and homeless and alone. The way she'd immediately pulled me inside, made me tea, and held me while I cried.

"Dawn and Mark didn't hesitate. They said I could stay with them as long as I needed to. They'd support me and take care of me through the pregnancy. They understood that I couldn't terminate it and would never pressure me to."

"They saved you."

"They saved both of us—me and the baby. For the first few months, I thought maybe I could do it. Maybe I could raise the baby on my own with their help. I got a job at a local diner, started saving money, and began planning for the future."

I paused, gathering courage for the hardest part of the story.

"But as my pregnancy progressed, reality set in. I was nineteen years old, with no education beyond high school, no real job prospects, and no family support except for Dawn and Mark. How could I provide for a child? How could I give her the life she deserved?"

"You started considering adoption."

I nodded. "It tore at my heart to even think about it, but I knew it might be the right thing to do. I started looking into agencies, meeting with counselors, trying to figure out the best option for the baby."

"What happened then?"

"Dawn came to me." A small smile crossed my lips despite everything. "She and Mark had been trying to have a baby for years without success. They'd been through fertility treatments, miscarriages, and adoptions that fell through. When Dawn saw how torn up I was about giving the baby to strangers, she made a suggestion that changed everything."

I could see JW already piecing together where this was going.

"She and Mark offered to adopt the baby. They said, that way, I could still be part of her life, watch her grow up, be involved in raising her even if I couldn't be her mother officially. No one would need to know I'd been pregnant—as far as anyone was concerned, Dawn and Mark had finally been granted a child."

"And you agreed?"

"Not right away. I agonized over it. Part of me still wanted to keep her, to find a way to make it work on my own. But the rational part of me knew my sister and her husband could give her stability, security, and a nurturing two-parent home with financial resources I couldn't provide."

The next part was the most painful to remember, and I had to take several deep breaths before I could continue.

"When I went into labor, Dawn was right there with me. Mark was too. They held my hands through every contraction, coached me through the delivery, and wept with me when Gisela was born." My voice caught. "She was the most gorgeous baby I'd ever seen. Perfect in every way. And when they placed her in my arms for the first time, I knew I was looking at a piece of you and a piece of me, combined into this precious little person."

JW's own eyes were wet now. "How long did you have with her?"

"Three days in the hospital. Dawn let me hold her, feed her, and rock her to sleep. She said it was important for me to have that time, to bond with her even though I wouldn't be able to keep her." I wiped my eyes. "On the third day, the social worker came with the adoption papers. I signed them while weeping, legally giving up all rights to my daughter."

"That must have been the hardest thing you've ever done."

"It was. But it was also the most selfless thing I could do for her. Dawn and Mark were incredible parents—are incredible parents. They gave Gisela everything I couldn't. A stable home, financial security, educational opportunities, unconditional care."

"And you got to watch her grow up."

"From a distance, yes. As Aunt Echo. Dawn made sure I was always part of her life. Birthday parties, school plays, soccer games, graduations. I was there for all of it, cherishing her fiercely but never able to tell her the truth about who I really was to her."

JW was quiet for a long moment, processing everything I'd told him. "What about the father? On her birth certificate, I mean."

"Unknown. I told Dawn I didn't know who the father was, that it had been a brief relationship with someone who'd left town. I never told anyone about you, never gave them your name or any details. I thought it was better that way."

"You protected me even then."

"I protected all of us. You, me, Gisela. The fewer people who knew the truth, the better it would be for her."

We sat in silence for several minutes, the weight of my confession settling between us. I waited for JW to process everything, to decide whether he could accept me after keeping this massive secret from him.

"I understand why you didn't tell me when we reconnected. When we started building something new together, how could you have explained all of this? How could you have told me I had a daughter who didn't know I existed?"

"I know you can never forgive me—"

He cupped my cheek. "No, Echo, you don't need my forgiveness. We were both bound by circumstances we couldn't control. We were both young and made the decisions we thought were best at the time." His gaze was intense and full of affection. "You were the one who was left alone, feeling abandoned. You faced an impossible situation with courage and grace, making the most selfless choice imaginable. You gave our daughter a wonderful life with people who could care for her properly."

"But I lied to you. I've been lying to you since the day we reconnected."

"You were protecting our daughter and protecting yourself. I understand that completely." His thumbs brushed away my tears. "What I can't fathom is how you've carried this burden alone for so long. The strength it must have required, the pain you've endured in silence."

His words broke down the last of my defenses, and I collapsed against him again, sobbing with relief and exhaustion and overwhelming gratitude for this man who somehow understood everything.

We held each other then, both grieving for the time we'd lost and the pain we'd both endured unnecessarily. As we lay, facing each other on top of the covers, he told me how stunning Gisela was, how he could see both of us in her.

"She's becoming a doctor," I said, pride filling my voice despite everything that had happened. "An oncologist, specializing in pediatric cancer. She's brilliant, JW. She always was, even as a little girl."

"Tell me about her. Tell me about our daughter."

So I did. I told him about Gisela's first steps, which she'd taken in Dawn's living room while I was visiting. Her first words, which had been "mama"—directed at Dawn, of course, but it had still made my heart swell. How she'd been an early reader, devouring books faster than my sister could buy them. Her soccer phase in middle school, when she'd been the fastest runner on her team. The way she'd excelled in science classes, particularly in biology and chemistry.

"She got a full scholarship to Stanford. Full ride, everything paid for. She graduated summa cum laude with a degree in biochemistry, then went straight into medical school."

"Following in her mother's footsteps. Dedicated to helping others."

"She's doing her residency at the children's hospital in Palo Alto now. Pediatric oncology is incredibly difficult—the toll of working with sick children is enormous—but she says it's her calling. She wants to be there for the families going through the worst time of their lives."

"Like you, her *mother*."

I shook my head. I wasn't. Dawn was.

"Tell me more about her," JW said, leaning forward to kiss my cheek. "I want to know everything."

"When she was in high school, she started volunteering with me at Miracles of Hope. She said watching me work with families inspired her to pursue medicine. If only she knew…"

"Perhaps she will soon."

Before I could respond, another knock came at my door. At the same time, I received a text from Kingston, saying he was outside.

My heart raced as I looked up at JW, panic probably written all over my expression. He squeezed my hand reassuringly and nodded toward the door.

"It's time," he said simply.

We walked to the front door together, and with trembling hands, I opened it. Outside stood Dawn, looking worried but compassionate. Kingston appeared confused but supportive. And Gisela.

"Can we come in?" Dawn asked gently.

I nodded, stepping aside to let them enter. The moment they were inside, Gisela moved straight to me, drawing me close exactly the way JW had done earlier.

"I know everything," she said softly, her voice thick with tears. "Mom told me. About the pregnancy, about the adoption, about why you've been my aunt instead of my mother all these years, and that JW is my father."

I started weeping again, my body shaking against hers. "Gisela, I'm so sorry. I'm so sorry I lied to you, that I kept this from you, that I—"

"Shh," she soothed, stroking my hair the same way I'd soothed her when she was little and she'd crawl into my lap. "You don't need to apologize. You have nothing to be sorry for."

"How can you say that? I've lied to you your entire life!"

She pulled back to look at me, her eyes—JW's eyes—brimming with tears. "You gave me the most incredible life, Echo. You gave me parents who cherished me, who supported my dreams, who gave me every opportunity to succeed. You sacrificed your own happiness for *me*."

"But I should have told you the truth. You had a right to know who I really was."

"I've always known who you really were. You were the woman who never missed a birthday party, who cheered louder than anyone at my soccer games, who helped me with science projects and college applications. You were the one who taught me about compassion and service to others. You were the one who inspired me to become a doctor."

I looked at her, hardly believing what I was hearing.

"You think I didn't notice how much you cared about me? How you lit up every time you saw me? How you knew exactly what to say when I was upset or scared?" She smiled through her own tears. "You were never just my aunt. I always felt a special connection to you that I couldn't explain."

"Gisela…"

"I pray that someday you can accept my gratitude instead of carrying guilt. I had a wonderful childhood and life because of your sacrifice, and I'm just so happy that we were able to be close."

She paused, looking beyond me to JW. "I became a doctor because of how much I respected and looked up to Aunt Echo. She showed me what it meant to dedicate your life to helping others, to being there for people in their darkest moments. That innate need to help others, I learned from watching her."

Over Gisela's shoulder, my eyes met Kingston's. He'd been standing quietly, taking everything in, but now, he stepped forward. He wrapped his arms around both Gisela and me, creating a three-way embrace that felt like a sanctuary.

"You don't owe anyone an apology. You have nothing to be sorry for," he said. "You're the best mother, the best person I know, and you did nothing wrong."

"You believed Gisela was your cousin, not your half sister," I whispered, pulling back to look at him.

He smiled through tears I'd rarely seen him shed. "She was always like a sister to me anyway. This just makes it official."

The simplicity of his acceptance, the complete lack of anger or resentment, overwhelmed me. Here were two young people who'd just discovered that their entire understanding of their family was built on a lie, and neither of them was angry with me for it.

"How are you both being so calm about this? How are you not furious with me for deceiving you?"

Dawn spoke up from where she'd been standing quietly by the door. "Because they understand care when they see it, Echo. They understand sacrifice. They know that everything you did was motivated by what was best for both of them."

I looked around the room at each of them—Gisela, Kingston, Dawn, then JW, the man I adored, who loved me despite my deceit.

In everyone's eyes, I saw acceptance. Not judgment, not anger, not resentment. Just pure, unconditional support.

JW stood and moved to my side, putting his hand around my shoulders and pulling me close to him. He leaned in and whispered in my ear, "I care about you more than life itself. All of you."

My eyes filled with fresh moisture, but these were different. These were tears of relief, of gratitude, of overwhelming joy. For the first time in twenty-eight years, I could breathe freely.

JW looked at his watch and smiled. "We're getting married in fifteen hours. Everyone best leave, so my bride and I can get the rest we need before our big day."

"You still want to marry me? Even after everything you've learned? Even knowing that I kept this from you?"

"Nothing would ever change that. If anything, knowing how strong you are, how much you've sacrificed for the people you care about, makes me cherish you even more."

Gisela, Dawn, and Kingston moved toward us, wrapping both JW and me in a group embrace.

"We'll see you in the morning," Dawn said, kissing my cheek. "This is going to be the most magical wedding."

After they left, the house felt different. Lighter. The secrets that had weighed me down for so long were finally gone, replaced by truth and acceptance.

JW took my hand and led me back to the bedroom. We undressed each other slowly, reverently, like we were discovering each other for the first time. When he kissed me, it tasted of forgiveness and new beginnings.

We made an intimate connection with a tenderness and passion that felt right because, now, there were no secrets between us, only honesty. Every touch was a promise, every kiss a vow, every whispered word of affection a commitment to the future we would build together.

For the first time in thirty years, I was completely free to give myself to the man I'd never stopped caring about. Tomorrow, I would marry him with my whole heart, knowing that our family—complicated and unconventional, as it was—was built on sacrifice and truth.

As I settled into sleep in JW's embrace, I thought about the dress hanging in my closet, about the vows I'd written, about the friends and family who would gather to witness our union. But mostly, I thought about how fortunate I was to have found my way back to this man, and how grateful we were to have discovered that love really could conquer anything.

Epilogue

JW

My wife and I stood on Elk Avenue hand-in-hand, watching the Independence Day parade where our eyes had met for the first time in thirty years. Where our second chance had begun. This year, it was a celebration of who and what we'd become. Happily married and at peace. Both of us. For the first time in either of our lives.

Echo stood beside me, her summer dress catching the morning light, her wedding ring glinting as she pointed out floats to the children who called us Grandma and Grandpa. The haunted look that had shadowed her features during our engagement was gone, replaced by the tranquility of a woman who no longer carried secrets.

"Grandpa JW, look!" Luna's voice cut through the crowd as she bounced between Victor and me, her small hands tugging at both our sleeves. The high school marching band was approaching, their brass instruments gleaming in the afternoon sun. At six years old, Luna's leukemia was now in remission, and watching her dance to the music with such unbridled joy never failed to make my heart swell.

"I see them, sweetheart," I said, hoisting her up onto my shoulders so she could get a better view over the crowd.

Down the sidewalk, I spotted the familiar chaos of the Wheaton family gathering. They'd staked out the same prime real estate they'd claimed last year. Flynn was doing her best to wrangle two-year-old Rowan and keep track of the twins, while Irish kept a protective hand on their seven-month-old baby boy, fast asleep in his carrier. They'd named him John William, but called him Willie.

Nearby, Buck and TJ were dealing with their own handful as five-year-old Buckaroo darted between the adults, clearly looking for his next adventure. Nearby, Holt swayed gently back and forth, cradling a sleeping Scarlet with one arm while the other was around Keltie's shoulders.

A little ways down, Cord and Juni had managed to find seats with Porter and Cici. Both Cici and Juni were expecting, their hands resting on their growing bellies that promised new additions to our family later in the year.

Echo and I had somehow become Grandma and Grandpa to this wonderful, chaotic bunch, and I couldn't imagine anything better.

"Glad I could be here this year," Bridger said, nodding toward Gisela, who was taking pictures with the enthusiasm of someone documenting her first small-town celebration. "She's having a blast."

Our daughter had flown in from California especially for the weekend, arranging her residency schedule around what she'd declared "an essential family gathering." Watching her laugh with Cord and Juni as they explained the parade's local history filled me with quiet pride.

The months since our wedding had brought a rhythm I'd never expected to find. We spent our summers here, in Crested Butte, me helping out at Roaring Fork while Echo trained Melanie to take over as Miracles of Hope's new director.

In winter, we spent more time at Sangre Vista, where we were building a house on what had become our favorite ridge to watch both the sunrise and sunset.

"She amazes me," Echo said, following my gaze to where Gisela was now showing Luna how to use her camera. "She's so patient with children."

"Gets that from her mother," I replied.

"Both of them," Echo corrected gently.

She was right. Dawn had raised Gisela with the same nurturing instincts Echo brought to every child she encountered through her charity work. Our daughter had been shaped by two remarkable women, and it showed in everything she did.

"The oncology program at Stanford is lucky to have her," Dawn, who stood beside us, added, pride evident in her voice. "Though I worry about the hours she keeps."

"All parents worry," Mark said with a gentle smile. "But she's doing exactly what she was meant to do."

"She says the work energizes her," Echo said. "Helping families through the worst moments of their lives—that's her calling."

I'd seen that dedication firsthand during Gisela's visits to New Mexico. She'd spent hours with me in the workshop, restoring an old piano while we talked about music and medicine and the strange paths that had brought us together. She called me by my name rather than any paternal title, but the bond between us grew stronger with each conversation.

After the parade ended, Echo and I walked two blocks over to the house she kept saying she should sell and I kept saying was our love nest. "Happy?" she asked when we walked in the front door.

"Completely."

"I'll just grab the cake, then we can go."

We were headed to the Roaring Fork for an afternoon of music and dancing, followed by a chuckwagon dinner and campfire.

The drive to the ranch took us along the same mountain roads where I'd first pursued her after she fled the night before our wedding, where we'd confronted decades of secrets and pain and emerged stronger for having faced the truth together.

As we pulled in, the whole crew stood waiting for us.

"We have been blessed with the most beautiful family, my love," I said, pulling Echo close as we looked over at parents and children who would grow up knowing their history and understanding the sacrifices that had brought them to this moment. In front of us stretched the valley where Patricia's dream of her children finding happiness had exceeded even her most optimistic hopes.

"Sometimes, I wonder if I'm dreaming," Echo murmured, leaning up to kiss my cheek. "We have quite a love story, JW."

She was right. It had taken thirty years to complete, but the best stories, I'd learned, were worth the wait.

Keep reading for a sneak peek at
the next book in Heather Slade's
Roaring Fork Ranch series,
Roaring Fork Bridger

He never got over losing her.
She never stopped loving him.
Together, they'll fake a reunion that
becomes all too real.

BRIDGER

When Lyric walks back into my life with questions
about my bulls acting strange, every protective instinct
I have kicks in—for my livelihood and for her. She
broke my heart when she left, but I never stopped
wanting to keep her safe. Now someone's targeting
everything I've built, and she might be the only person
who can help me figure out who. The problem is, working together means pretending we're back together,
and with Lyric, I've never been good at pretending.

LYRIC

I've been covering rodeos long enough to know when
something's wrong, but approaching Bridger about it

means facing the man I never got over. Walking away from him was the hardest thing I've ever done, but I had my reasons. Now we need each other to uncover the truth about what's happening to the sport we both love. Going undercover as a couple should be simple—except nothing about my feelings for this cowboy has ever been simple.

Prologue

Bridger

The gravel crunched under our boots as we crossed the motel parking lot. Lyric walked beside me, talking with her hands the way she always did after a good night at the rodeo.

It had been three years since we'd been together, but some things never changed—especially Lyric.

Fuck if I didn't miss her, though. The woman drove me crazy in every way possible. Whether it was the way she'd beleaguer a point until I gave in just to shut her up, or her naked body under mine as we shared the best sex I'd ever had in my life.

But we were ancient history now. Had been since the morning I'd woken up to find her gone, bags packed, saying she had big dreams to chase and I wasn't one of them.

Now, we were friends. Had to be given the rodeo community was tight-knit and we saw each other at events that took place one weekend after another. Every so often we'd grab drinks or dinner. Sometimes with a big group alone, or other times alone, like tonight.

When we reached the split between room nine and twelve, she stopped.

"You know I don't need an escort, right?" she said, motioning to the lower-numbered rooms. "I'm perfectly capable of handling thirty feet of sidewalk."

I paused, key card in hand. "Never said you weren't."

She flashed that grin that had always spelled trouble. "Good night, Bridger."

"Night, Lyric."

I unlocked my door but didn't go inside. Instead, I leaned against the frame and watched her. Old habits. She had her key card out, reaching for the handle, when she froze.

The scream that tore from her throat sent ice through my veins.

I was running before my brain caught up, crossing the distance between us in seconds. She stood completely still outside her room, staring into the darkness beyond.

"Stay here." I pushed past her to go inside.

"Like hell I'm staying out here." She was right behind me as I took the first tentative step, then hit the light switch.

The place was destroyed. Drawers dumped, clothes scattered, her laptop bag ripped open and empty. Whoever had done this had been thorough.

And angry.

"Bridger." Her voice sounded nothing like the ball-buster Lryic Simmons I knew.

"What?"

"In here."

I looked to where she was pointing in the direction of the bathroom. I looked over her shoulder and there, written across the mirror in her own red lipstick, was a short but brutal message.

STOP DIGGING OR YOU'RE DEAD.

About the Author

USA Today best-selling author Heather Slade writes shamelessly sexy, edge-of-your seat romantic suspense.

She gave herself the gift of writing a book for her own birthday one year. Sixty-plus books later (and counting), she's having the time of her life.

The women Slade writes are self-confident, strong, with wills of their own, and hearts as big as the Colorado sky. The men are sublimely sexy, seductive alphas who rise to the challenge of capturing the sweet soul of a woman whose heart they'll hold in the palm of their hand forever. Add in a couple of neck-snapping twists and turns, a page-turning mystery, and a swoon-worthy HEA, and you'll be holding one of her books in your hands.

She loves to hear from her readers. You can contact her at heather@heatherslade.com

To keep up with her latest news and releases, please visit her website at www.heatherslade.com to sign up for her newsletter.

MORE FROM AUTHOR HEATHER SLADE

ROMANTIC SUSPENSE

K19 SECURITY SOLUTIONS TEAM ONE
Razor's Edge
Gunner's Redemption
Mistletoe's Magic
Mantis' Desire
Dutch's Salvation

K19 SECURITY SOLUTIONS TEAM TWO
Striker's Choice
Monk's Fire
Halo's Oath
Tackle's Honor
Onyx's Awakening

K19 SHADOW OPERATIONS TEAM ONE
Code Name: Ranger
Code Name: Diesel
Code Name: Wasp
Code Name: Cowboy
Code Name: Mayhem

K19 ALLIED INTELLIGENCE TEAM ONE
Code Name: Ares
Code Name: Cayman
Code Name: Poseidon
Code Name: Zeppelin
Code Name: Magnet

K19 ALLIED INTELLIGENCE TEAM TWO
Code Name: Puck
Code Name: Michelangelo
Code Name: Typhon
Code Name: Hornet
Code Name: Reaper

K19 GENESIS CONSORTIUM TEAM ONE
Blackjack's Ascent
Dagger's Shield
Sundance's Trail
Nomad's Compass
Preacher's Decree

K19 SENTINEL CYBER TEAM ONE
Code Name: Admiral
Code Name: Dante
Code Name: Grit
Code Name: Tank
Code Name: Atticus

K19 SENTINEL CYBER TEAM TWO
Code Name: Kodiak
Code Name: Paragon
Code Name: Vex
Code Name: Shredder
Code Name: Jagger

PROTECTORS UNDERCOVER TEAM ONE
Undercover Agent
Undercover Emissary
Undercover Savior
Undercover Infidel
Undercover Shadow

ROYAL AGENTS OF MI6
Make Me Shiver
Drive Me Wilder
Feel My Pinch
Chase My Shadow
Find My Angel

THE INVINCIBLES TEAM ONE
Code Name: Deck
Code Name: Edge
Code Name: Grinder
Code Name: Rile
Code Name: Smoke

THE INVINCIBLES TEAM TWO
Code Name: Buck
Code Name: Irish
Code Name: Saint
Code Name: Hammer
Code Name: Rip

THE UNSTOPPABLES TEAM ONE
Code Name: Fury
Code Name: Merried

MORE FROM AUTHOR HEATHER SLADE

WINE COUNTRY ROMANCE

BUTLER RANCH

Kade's Worth
Brodie's Promise
Maddox's Truce
Naughton's Secret
Mercer's Vow
Kade's Return
Butler Ranch Christmas

WICKED WINEMAKERS CENTRAL COAST FIRST LABEL

Brix's Bid
Ridge's Release
Press' Passion
Zin's Sins
Tryst's Temptation

WICKED WINEMAKERS CENTRAL COAST SECOND LABEL

Beau's Beloved
Cru's Crush
Bit's Bliss
Snapper's Seduction
Kick's Kiss

WICKED WINEMAKERS RUSSIAN RIVER VALLEY FIRST LABEL

Bas' Blend
Hux's Harvest
Wolf's Want
Oak's Vintage
Cooper's Claim

COWBOY ROMANCE

COWBOYS OF CRESTED BUTTE

A Cowboy Falls
A Cowboy's Dance
A Cowboy's Kiss
A Cowboy Stays
A Cowboy Wins

ROARING FORK RANCH

Roaring Fork Wrangler
Roaring Fork Roughstock
Roaring Fork Rockstar
Roaring Fork Rooker
Roaring Fork Bridger

SANGRE VISTA RANCH

Thorn's Stand
Stetson's Storm
Maverick's Reckoning
Cinch's Wager
Flints Chance

HEATHER SLADE WRITING AS
MERRIGAN CALDER

DARK ROMANCE
THORNED THISTLE
Commanded

Possessed

Obsessed

Captured

Surrendered

NEW SERIES COMING SOON
CRIMSON CHALICE
VELVET VIPER

www.ingramcontent.com/pod-product-compliance
Lightning Source LLC
Chambersburg PA
CBHW071344300726
48976CB00006B/1762